ACES AND EIGHTS AND DEAD WEREWOLF DATES

JODI VAUGHN

NEWSLETTER SIGN UP!

CHAPTER 1

*B*eing a vampire sucked.

I was drained by the sun.

I was addicted to drinking blood.

I was cursed to walk the Earth for eternity.

At least until someone staked me. Or cut off my head. Whichever.

I stumbled into the kitchen. The sun was not up yet, but I could feel my energy starting to wane with the impending daylight. I tightened the tie on my robe and plopped onto a barstool. I pulled yesterday's newspaper closer and unfolded it.

Just because I was a vampire, didn't mean I could become less aware of the latest news in Charming, Mississippi.

It had been a few weeks since the murder of Memphis, the country singer, who happened to be Khalan's Maker. Khalan was *my* Maker. She had kidnapped my girls, and Khalan had tried to rescue them. In the end, I'd had to rescue them all. Khalan had killed Memphis to make sure she could never hurt my girls or me again. She might have been a country singer with the body of a supermodel, but she was crazy evil in the head.

I was glad she was dead.

One less thing to worry about.

Khalan continued to come every Friday night to take me to feed. I never killed anyone, just took enough blood to satisfy my thirst.

Since my divorce from Miles, I had gotten a job with Stan who was a private investigator. He owned Discrete P.I. Agency. I was his photographer, who caught people cheating on their spouses or defrauding their insurance companies. I took the job after I had found out that my ex-husband was struggling to pay both alimony and child support. It wouldn't have bothered me so much, except for the fact that my daughters had to visit him in his squalid apartment above Mrs. Grishom's garage.

I couldn't bear to have them in that kind of environment.

So, I had requested the courts to lower the alimony since I was making my own money, taking pictures for Stan.

If not for my girls, I wouldn't have done that. After the hell he'd put me through by having an affair with my best friend, Nikki, he didn't deserve any leniency.

But that was the least of my problems. My current being that I was a single mom of two beautiful girls, and I was a fairly recently turned vampire. The night I'd discovered Miles and Nikki in our bed, I had also been nearly beheaded by a snowplow and turned into a vampire by my Maker, Khalan.

The upside being that becoming a vampire had literally turned back the hands of time on my face and, most impressively, my ass. Instead of looking like my thirty-five years of age, I now looked like a young twenty-three-year-old. My friends were constantly asking who my plastic surgeon was. I told them it was Botox.

In exchange for my immortal life, I now had to keep the balance and maintain my identity to everyone I knew. It'd been hard, especially when I knew my Maker didn't really like me all that much.

"Mom, I have a problem." Arianna eased onto a barstool at the kitchen island. I looked up from the morning paper, a little taken aback. I glanced at the time on the clock.

It was Saturday morning, and she wasn't sleeping in. More astonishingly, asking for my advice. Something she hadn't done much since becoming a teenager.

"Tell me so I can help." I folded the newspaper I had been reading and laid it to the side on the island.

I held my breath. Was this about clothing? That new boy in her class? Or had she somehow discovered what I really was: a vampire?

Arianna glanced down at her hands folded in her lap and looked back at me.

I had a feeling it was something big.

"You can tell me anything." I gave her an encouraging smile.

She nodded and looked up at me. "I hate to tell you this, but Dad is dating someone."

I felt the wind rush out of my lungs.

We had been divorced for months now. But, deep down in my heart, I didn't like it. I could never comprehend how a father could move on so easily from his family. That was something I would have to deal with, not him.

"I see." I pressed my hands against the kitchen island and chose my next words carefully.

"Well, honey, you know that we are no longer married. Your dad is free to date whoever he wants."

Arianna cocked her head at me. "Aren't you curious who she is?"

Honestly, I was dying to know. But I didn't want to show

her that. I was trying to raise two strong, independent girls, so I needed to show that same strong independence in myself.

"You're taking this better than I expected. You aren't dating anyone, are you?" She narrowed her eyes a little at me.

I felt my eyes bulge. "Me?" I laughed and shook my head. "I don't really have time for dating right now, honey." I reached for the newspaper.

Her face fell a little. "That's what I thought you were going to say. Mom, I don't want you to put your life on hold for me and Gabby."

"What are you talking about? Do you not realize you guys are my life?" I smoothed her dark hair out of her eyes and smiled. I couldn't believe how much taller she had gotten over the past few months. In another few years, she would be out of high school and into college.

"What I mean to say, Mom, is that Daddy is moving on with his life. He's dating, and he seems to be happy. What I'm trying to say is I want you to start dating again, too. It won't be long before you're an empty-nester. And God knows me and Gabby would be happier if you had someone to look after you after we're gone. And I can't have you coming up to college every weekend." She gave me a playful smile.

"Ole Miss is not that far from here, you know?" I could totally visit every weekend.

Her smile faded. "Yeah. About that. I wanted to talk to you about colleges, too."

"Okay, I'm sure you won't have any problems getting into Ole Miss since your father went there," I said brightly.

"What if I don't want to go to Ole Miss?"

I was speechless. Since Arianna was a child, she'd always loved going to college football games with us. She'd said that was where she wanted to go to school.

"What do you mean?"

"I've been doing a lot of research online, and we've had a lot of recruiters at the school. Well, I spoke to the recruiter for Alabama..."

"Roll Tide?" My mouth dropped. Miles hated Alabama with a vengeance. "Really?"

"Yeah."

"But aren't a lot of your friends going to Ole Miss? I mean, it's not like you have to decide now. You still have a few more years before you graduate."

"I know." She looked up at me. "It's just Alabama has a spectacular program, and they offer so many things..."

"What about your friends?"

"Sometimes, it's good to make new friends, those that will help you grow and achieve goals."

I nodded. She was right. I couldn't help but wonder if going to Alabama was a way to start over with people who didn't know anything about Miles' indiscretion.

"You are right about that. Keep looking into it, and we will discuss it with your dad."

Arianna sighed. "Dad isn't going to be happy."

"Your father wants you to be happy at the college of your choosing. We'll have to look into scholarship requirements and tuition and all of that..."

"Really?" Her face brightened like a million rising suns.

"Absolutely." I smiled.

She jumped up and threw her arms around my neck. "Thank you, Mom. I love you."

"I love you, too." I pulled her back and looked into her eyes. "But remember, we still have to discuss it with your father."

"I know. What if he won't pay for the tuition if I go there?" She worried her lip with her teeth.

"Then you'd better get a scholarship. You've got the grades. Just keep them up."

"Thanks, Mom." She gave me another hug and raced to her room.

I rested my chin in the palm of my hand and smiled. Miles would certainly be disappointed. That cheered me considerably.

After the divorce, I had been so concerned about my girls. I worried I was messing things up for them and their future by not staying with Miles.

But now, seeing Arianna excited about college and new challenges, I knew they would both be okay.

And having Miles upset that his firstborn wasn't going to follow in his footsteps and attend his alma mater, well…that was icing on the cake.

I pulled into the parking lot off Main Street. My boss, Uncle Stan, who owned Discrete P.I. Agency, had called the night before and told me to come in first thing in the morning. I figured he was going to give me a new assignment. The last big case I had done for him was catching an abusive husband cheating on his wife. The wife had hired Discrete P.I. so she could get a divorce without getting shunned by her church. In the end, her husband had given her what she wanted.

It had been an exciting case, but lately, my projects had been pretty boring. I had two cases where I had to get pictures of people who were defrauding insurance companies. Somebody claimed injuries so they could draw disability but, in actuality, they were faking it. I had also gotten some pictures of cheating husbands, but nothing very dramatic.

I wasn't complaining. So far, the work had been steady, and the money great.

I opened the door of the dated building housing Uncle

Stan's office. I pushed the button for the elevator and glanced at my reflection in the shiny metal doors.

The elevator dinged, and I entered the cab and pressed a button.

I ascended to the correct floor.

As soon as the doors slid open, I headed straight to Uncle Stan's office and opened the door.

He'd told me once that he'd had a secretary but fired her because he didn't like anyone else in his business. He pretty much answered the phones, talked with clients, and handled the bookkeeping.

I looked at Uncle Stan, who was seated behind his messy desk. Stacks of brown folders sat on the worn mahogany surface, and Post-it Notes clung to the black filing cabinet behind him. The clutter and disorder gave me anxiety.

"Hi, Uncle Stan. What did you want to talk to me about?" I eased into the seat across from him.

"Rachel, how many times do I have to tell you to call me Stan. I'm not your uncle." He looked at me over his glasses.

"I know. But I can't help it. It's habit." I shrugged. I had met Stan through my good friend. In reality, he was *her* uncle, and she always introduced him to everyone as *Uncle Stan*.

He stared at me from across his desk. "I need to tell you something, Rachel. You don't know this, but your friend Nikki came to see me a while back."

"Ex-friend. Nikki is my ex-friend." I glared.

He nodded and held up his hand. "My bad. Your ex-friend Nikki hired me. I think it's time you knew since you are my employee."

"Hired you for what?" I gave him my best innocent expression. He had no idea I'd followed Nikki to his office late one night. I'd snuck up to the office and overheard the whole conversation.

"She hired me to find her husband, Brad." He stopped shuffling the paper clutter on his desk and looked at me.

"Find Brad? But I thought he left a suicide note." I schooled my expression into one of confusion. Since becoming a vampire, I was learning to be an expert. "Isn't he dead?"

"He did leave a note. But since there's no body, Nikki hired me to find it." He shrugged.

"Nikki seems to think that Brad might still be alive. Or at the very least, she's hoping he really is dead so she can collect on his life insurance. That's why she hired me. Seems she needs that money really bad." He sniffed and shoved his glasses up his nose.

"I don't understand. Why would she still entertain the idea that he is alive? He left a suicide note."

"Supposedly." Stan shuffled some papers on his desk.

My stomach clenched.

I swallowed hard.

Did Stan know more than he was letting on?

"So, why are you telling me this? It doesn't really concern me."

He steepled his hands in front of him on the desk and looked me square in the eyes. "The truth of the matter is that you are the best photographer that I've ever had. You do your job at night without complaint. Other photographers I've had complained about sleep deprivation and doing things they didn't want to do. But not you. You seem to thrive at night. And so far, I've not had any complaints. I'm telling you this out of professional courtesy."

I relaxed back in my chair and smiled. "Thank you for the compliment."

"You're welcome. And just so you know, I don't hand out compliments freely."

"I appreciate that." I did. It had been a while since

someone had given me a compliment. I smiled and relaxed in my seat.

"Now, back to the Nikki situation. I've had my best private investigators on the case for months. They cannot find any evidence to suggest where Brad Stollings might have gone. No trace of his truck. No sign of him. No activity on his credit or debit cards." He sighed heavily. "For all intents and purposes, it appears that he really did commit suicide."

I felt myself visibly relax and nodded.

"But until I find a body, I can't stop looking."

I wanted to roll my eyes and scream. Why couldn't he just leave it alone?

"I see."

"There's more. I want you to get some information for me."

"Me?" My mouth literally dropped open. "But I'm not an investigator. I'm a photographer." I crossed my arms.

"Yes. A damn good one. But you were close to Nikki and, by extension, her husband. You would know his habits, his haunts, where he would go if he got into a tight situation. Plus, you know Nikki better than anyone."

"Or so I thought." I snorted. "Didn't think she'd sleep with my husband. So, apparently, I didn't really know her at all."

He leveled a gaze at me.

"If you don't think he committed suicide, what do you think happened to him?" I leaned forward.

He looked at me and shoved his glasses up his nose again and then folded his hands on the desk. "My honest opinion?"

I nodded.

"From my experience, I believe Mr. Brad Stollings is dead. But I don't think he killed himself."

"What?" I thought my heart had stopped in my chest.

Did Uncle Stan know? Was he playing with me like a

mouse? Stringing me along until I spilled the beans about what had really happened?

"But..."

He held up his hand, stopping me from saying anything else. "Rachel, I know this may come as a surprise, but from everything I've heard about Brad, I have a lot of reasons to believe that someone killed the man. I think we are looking at a case of murder."

*a*fter I got back from Uncle Stan's, I went home and to sleep. I got six solid hours of rest, but I still felt tired.

I plopped down on the couch and grabbed my cell phone then dialed my friend Gina Randle.

She answered on the third ring.

"Hello?"

"Hi, Gina, do you have time for a talk?"

"Sure. Just give me one second." I could hear the ruffle and shuffle of papers. Gina was the operations manager for her husband's investment company.

She was by far one of the most self-disciplined people I knew.

"Are you sure? You sound kind of busy."

"Let's talk. I just got out of a meeting. This will be a nice distraction."

I thought for a second, carefully choosing my words. "Arianna mentioned that Miles is dating someone."

"Please tell me you're not jealous. I can hear the disappointment in your voice."

"I'm not jealous."

"Are you sure? Because all the women in Charming look up to you. We have a lot riding on you, Rachel."

I laughed. "Well, if you're counting on me, you guys are going to be disappointed." I lay back on the couch with the phone pressed to my ear and stifled a yawn.

"Are you kidding? You've done more for strong women than anyone else I know. So, what's up?"

"ARIANNA SAID that she's worried about me. Said that I should be dating. She says she doesn't want me to be alone after she and Gabby go off to college." I pressed my fingers to my temple and groaned. "I think it's too soon, right?"

"To start dating? I was kind of hoping you'd bring that up. I've been meaning to talk to you about that."

"Really?" I frowned.

"Yes, but I didn't want to pressure you like some of the other girls. I know that Judith has been wanting to set you up with her husband's friend from work." Gina snorted. "But don't do it. He's twenty years older than you. You don't need to be with an old man." Gina paused. "Unless he has a butt-load of money."

I bit my lip. If she only knew how much older Khalan was, she would freak out.

"So, what do you think? Is Arianna right? Do I need to start dating?" I rubbed my temple again.

"I think it's ironic that you brought it up."

"Why?"

"Because I just so happen to have something that you might be interested in. It's called the Aces and Eights Dating for Charity Event. Our company is partnering with a few others in town to host it."

13

"What exactly is it? It isn't some kind of auction where you bid on a half-naked guy, is it?"

"No. But that's a great idea for next year."

"Gina…" I warned.

"No, seriously. It's a chance for you to see what's out there in the dating pond. You know, dip your toe in."

"How does it work?" I sat up and clutched a pillow to my stomach. Just talking about dating was giving me a stomachache.

"All the participants have to apply and pay a fee. People go through a vetting system, so not just anyone can attend. The best part of this whole thing is that it will take place on a riverboat on the Mississippi."

"What?" I sat up. Brad's body was at the bottom of the Mississippi River. It was the last place I wanted to be.

"The dress code is black-tie. There will be dinner, as well as an opportunity to gamble."

I could hear the excitement in Gina's voice.

"I don't know, Gina. I'm not much of a gambler."

"Sure, you are. You took a gamble when you left your marriage instead of sticking it out to save face."

"Not exactly what I meant."

"I know. But it will be fun. Plus, there are slot machines if you don't want to play poker."

"How do I know I won't end up with a serial killer?"

"There are no serial killers in Charming." Gina snorted.

"You are forgetting about Cal."

"Technically, he only killed the one girl…unless you know something I don't."

"I don't." I rubbed my hand across my face.

"Look. It will be fun. You get to dress up, play some poker, have a nice dinner…and maybe find someone nice who wants to take you on a date."

"I don't think I want the whole town of Charming knowing that I'm on a date."

"Well, here's the best part. They don't have to know. The questionnaire is very detailed, so you will be matched with someone who has similar things in common. Plus you have to have a login to get into the website. Besides, all the proceeds from the event go to the Domestic Abuse Charity for women."

"What if I get paired with some bald guy with bad breath that drives a clunker?"

"Well, here's the thing. The tickets are expensive. And, as I mentioned, there is a vetting process. And they do a background check, of course."

"So, how did your company come up with the idea?" I had to admit, the concept was very original.

"One of the guys here just got divorced after fifty years of marriage. He's been complaining that he can't find anybody his age that likes to do the things he does or who isn't looking for a sugar daddy. He says he's looking for good conversation and a woman with her own career who can go out to dinner every now and then. You know, some companionship."

"So, this is not a booty call thing?" I sighed.

GINA LAUGHED. "Definitely not. It's for women and men who are looking for a companion. Maybe a dinner date or perhaps a quick trip to the Florida Keys."

I grimaced. There was a time when I would have loved a quick trip to the Keys, but since becoming a vampire, I preferred cooler places with less sunlight. Like Antarctica.

"So, are you in?"

"I don't know, Gina." I pinched the bridge of my nose.

"There're only so many weekends you can stay home

alone when Miles has the girls. Just try it. You don't have to fall in love with anybody, and it will give you a great excuse to get out of the house."

"I don't just stay in the house. I do have a job now."

"Yeah, at night. When you should be dating. How's the job going, by the way?"

"It's going, which is great since I petitioned the court to lower Miles' alimony. Although now I'm wondering if I should've done that, considering he doesn't seem to be in too much of a financial bind anymore. He's back in his penthouse and has a new car."

"Told you not to do that."

"Yeah, I know. But I did it months ago when he was living in a roach-infested apartment above Mrs. Grishom's garage. I couldn't let the girls stay there with him."

"I understand, Rachel. But you need to treat yourself once in a while. You need to get in the game."

I sighed. "Okay, fine. I'll do it. Send me the application."

"Yay!" Gina squealed. "I'm so glad. And trust me, Rachel. You will not regret this."

She ended the call, and I buried my face in my hands.

Little did she know I already regretted it.

*M*iles had picked up the girls after school since it was his weekend to have them. I didn't have any work from Uncle Stan, so I cleaned the house like a madwoman.

Afterwards, I relaxed on the couch, ready to watch a movie. I picked up the remote. A sense of sadness washed over me.

Maybe Gina and Arianna were right. Perhaps I did need to try and find someone, even if it was only temporary.

I had just clicked on the TV when my cell phone rang.

"Hello?"

"Mrs. Jones?" An unfamiliar male voice had me looking at the time.

It was way too late for a sales pitch or a political call.

"Yes?"

"My name is Dr. Kramer. I am Cal Dennery's psychiatrist."

I froze.

"Yes?"

"I'm sorry to call so late. But it's regarding Cal's case." He hesitated for a second. "And it concerns your part in it."

"My part?" I stood up. "I had nothing to do with what Cal did to that girl."

He chuckled softly. It sent chills up my spine.

"I wouldn't be quite so sure about that, Mrs. Jones."

"What is that supposed to mean?" I snapped. I was a lot of things, but a killer wasn't one of them. Not yet.

"Apparently, you've not talked to Carla lately."

I ran to the window and pulled aside the curtain, glancing across the street to my neighbor's house. Her garage door was down, and I didn't see any lights on inside. What was he talking about?

"Mrs. Jones, I just finished hypnotizing Cal. And I was quite surprised at what he said during our little session."

My anger melted into hard, cold fear. I dropped the curtain. I turned around and slid to the floor. I pressed the phone against my ear so hard, it began to hurt.

"You hypnotized him?" I'd thought both Carla and Cal had decided against hypnotism.

"Surprisingly enough, Cal started to remember the night of the murder. And do you know whose name he kept calling out?"

No, no, no.

"Ironically enough, it was yours."

"I have no clue why he would say my name," I said emphatically. "I barely knew Cal."

"It is of the utmost importance that you come to my office tomorrow."

"But it's Saturday. Aren't doctors' offices normally closed on Saturdays?"

"I'm making an exception, Rachel." He dropped the formality. In a sense, he was letting me know who was in charge.

"I don't know…" I really needed to talk to Khalan.

"This isn't a suggestion. Something is going on with my patient, and it has everything to do with you, Rachel."

I could feel all the blood drain from my face.

"I need you to meet me at my office tomorrow at seven a.m. I know how you prefer early hours versus daytime hours."

Holy shit.

He knew. He had to know that I was a vampire.

I swallowed hard, carefully considering my next words.

"Seven is fine. But I really don't think I can add anything helpful to the case." I tried to keep my voice nonchalant. But deep down inside, I was filled with a sense of terror and fear, unlike anything I'd ever known.

"Tomorrow it is, Mrs. Jones. Look forward to seeing you."

*K*halan pressed a glass of warm blood into my hand. I didn't even ask where he'd gotten it from. I didn't care.

After the phone call with Dr. Kramer, I'd called Khalan, telling him that I couldn't go out and feed tonight.

"You're going to have to kill him." He sat on the couch and gave me a hard look.

"The psychiatrist?" So far in my vampiric career, I had not managed to kill anyone—except for a raccoon, which was totally an accident on my part. I still carried a considerable amount of guilt over that.

"Not the doctor. Cal. You have to kill Cal." He shrugged.

I choked on my blood. "What?" I wiped my chin.

"Cal is the problem. Apparently, he remembered that you glamoured him. He's probably told the psychiatrist that you are a vampire and that you took blood from him. So, if he's dead, there's no one else with evidence that you are a vampire. Problem solved." He shrugged.

"But what about the psychiatrist?"

"You can kill him, too, but I think once Cal's out of the

way, Dr. Kramer won't risk his career by accusing a house-wife of being a vampire."

"This is getting way too complicated." I rubbed my fore-head and took another drink of the warm blood. "This is pretty good. Where did you get it?"

"Same place as always. Those vampire role-players. I just got it to go."

"They do that?"

"For me, they do." A slow smile crossed his lips.

"Funny." I took another drink. "Do all cities have fast food for vampires?"

"Every place I've lived does."

"How many times have you moved?"

He leaned back against the couch and looked up at the ceiling. "Four hundred and seventy-five, no... seventy-six times."

"Holy shit."

He shrugged. "Rachel, you can only live for so many years in the same town or city before people realize you're not getting any older. I mean, how are you going to explain to your grandchildren that Grandma doesn't age?"

I ran my finger around the rim of the glass and looked at him. "I've actually given that some thought. I figured I could take a class in theater makeup and maybe learn how to apply some wrinkles or age spots. Or, I can even get somebody to make a synthetic mask that I can put on when I'm around people."

"Well, you are going to need a bodysuit so your ass doesn't look like a twenty-five-year-old's."

I grinned. I was grateful for the compliment. Being thirty-five and looking twenty-five was one of the perks of being a vampire.

"Back to the problem at hand. I have to see the psychia-trist tomorrow. He wants me to meet him at seven."

"Don't go." Khalan narrowed his eyes.

"I have to. I get the feeling he'll badger me until I agree to talk to him. Plus, I need to see what I'm up against."

"Are you crazy? You will say something that'll incriminate you, and you'll be dragged into this case. Which you realize will be during the day. They're not going to have night court for Cal's trial. It's going to be straight up during the day. When you're at your weakest."

"Khalan, I'm not stupid."

"I didn't say you were. But you do get emotional. You need to learn to control that."

"So you've been telling me." I took another drink. I studied him over my glass of blood.

It had been a while since he killed his Maker, Memphis. Memphis had kidnapped my children in order to find Khalan. When I found them, Arianna and Gabby were in her tour bus bed, bleeding. And Khalan had been nailed to the wall, crucifix-style. We managed to get away, and Khalan killed his Maker to ensure that she wouldn't come back and find us. Before her death, Memphis had told me about Khalan's past.

Before he had been turned, Khalan had been married with family on the way. What was more incredulous was that he had been a preacher.

Khalan narrowed his eyes on me. "Just ask. It drives me crazy when you sit there with your little mouse spinning around on the wheel in your head, thinking of all those questions." He groaned.

I ignored the insult but took the invitation. I leaned forward. "So, you were married?"

"Yes." His voice was quiet.

"You didn't always hate people. I mean, you were a country preacher, right?"

"So it would seem."

Memphis had told me that she'd turned Khalan against his will when he rejected her advances. Memphis, being the selfish bitch she was, wanted what she wanted. And what she wanted was Khalan. In order to get him, she'd had to get the wife and child out of the way. She'd compelled and glamoured Khalan into killing his pregnant wife and unborn child. Khalan had lived for centuries with the guilt of murdering his family. His past made me understand him a little bit better. It made sense why he was so much more comfortable around animals than humans.

I set my glass on the coffee table and sat beside him on the sofa.

I gently placed my hand on his shoulder. He trained his gaze there and then looked me in the eyes.

"You know, Khalan, *she* forced you to do what you did. You shouldn't carry the guilt of this for eternity. It wasn't your fault."

His eyes hardened. "Do you see why I insisted that you come away from here? It's not that I want to tear you away from your family. I'm trying to protect them." He looked away. "You have a chance to watch them grow old and have children and grandchildren. From afar."

I drew my hand away and looked at him in surprise. "I guess I never really thought about it like that."

When I first became a vampire after Khalan had turned me, he'd insisted that I leave my family behind and live with him so I could learn how to survive.

As a mother of two girls, I could never see myself without my children. I'd insisted that I could live my life here in Charming, Mississippi, and still care for my children.

"You know I would never hurt my kids."

He gave a mirthless laugh. "I said the same thing. I thought I loved my wife dearly. So much so that I would never be able to harm her. But when you have your power

23

taken away from you by the hands of a Master vampire, you can't control anything."

"Then I'm lucky I have you as my Master."

"Don't be. You don't know what I'm capable of. What would you do if a stronger vampire came along and compelled you to do something to harm your family?"

Fear tightened its hand on my throat. "Is that possible? Can someone other than my Maker take control of me?"

"I don't know, Rachel. But I do know there are rumors of stronger vampires than Memphis. Those who have been around for thousands of years."

"Have you seen one?"

"No, but I've kept on the move, and I don't associate with other vampires. I keep to myself."

He stood and walked to the door.

"Be careful, Rachel," he said over his shoulder before he opened the door. "Don't let the psychiatrist get the best of you."

CHAPTER 6

I was a nervous ball of energy all freaking night. I couldn't stop thinking about my meeting with Cal's psychiatrist. I had tried to call Carla, but got no answer. I kept an eye on her house all night and never saw the lights come on. I wondered if she was out of town, or just hiding from me so she wouldn't have to answer any questions.

I tapped my finger on the steering wheel as I neared my destination. The last time I had seen Carla and Cal together was when I had gone to see him at the jail after Carla had asked me to go with her. I had convinced them both that hypnosis was a bad idea. I'd used the theory that people who'd been hypnotized later claimed that they had been abducted by aliens. The reality was that I was afraid the psychiatrist would put something in Cal's head that wasn't true. Or that Cal would remember me drinking blood from him and out me as a vampire.

I'd thought I had convinced them not to do the hypnosis.

Apparently, they'd changed their minds.

I pulled into the parking lot of the medical offices. I didn't know Dr. Kramer and figured he must be new to town. As a former doctor's wife, I thought I knew every doctor in Charming.

I grabbed my purse and slid out of the car. I wore my large, oversized sunglasses and my new Fedora. Since becoming a vampire, hats were now a necessary accessory.

The sound of my heels clicking against the asphalt was unusually loud in my ears. I took a deep breath and opened the door to the building.

"May I help you?" The older secretary immediately greeted me with a smile.

"Yes. I'm here to see Dr. Kramer." I took off my glasses and dropped them in my purse.

"Of course." She nodded. "He said he had an early consultation with a Mrs. Jones." She stood from behind her desk. "If you will just follow me."

I followed her down a hallway to an office. She knocked softly.

"Come in, Mrs. Wilson."

She smiled and opened the door. "Mrs. Jones is here to see you." She waved me in.

I lifted my head and squared my shoulders in a confident stance. I wasn't about to be bullied into saying something that would put me in jeopardy.

"Mrs. Jones." Dr. Kramer, a short, fat man with oversized lips, stood from behind his desk. "Please, come in. Would you like some coffee?"

Mrs. Wilson waited for directions.

"No, thank you." I smiled pleasantly.

"Really? Not a coffee drinker? Perhaps your tastes run to something different." He arched his eyebrow.

"I would love some English Breakfast tea if you have it," I added. I didn't want to give him any more ammunition than he already had.

"Of course. Mrs. Wilson, if you would be so kind." He

nodded at the secretary.

"Right away." She left the room.

"Please, have a seat." Dr. Kramer motioned me towards the chair across the desk. I eased myself into the wingback chair and placed my purse in my lap.

"You don't see many people wearing hats anymore." He nodded at my Fedora.

"Dr. Kramer, I can tell from your accent that you are not from around here. If you were, then you would certainly see a lot of Southern women sporting hats." I shrugged and patted my hat in place.

"Of course. Of course." He smiled and nodded. "I meant no disrespect. The look suits you."

I looked up when Mrs. Wilson re-entered the office with a hot cup of tea.

"I brought a packet of sugar, but we seem to be out of cream," she said.

"Not a problem. I love my tea without anything in it." I took a quick sip and smiled. "It's perfect."

Mrs. Wilson smiled broadly and left the room. She shut the door behind her.

I took another sip of my tea and then set the mug down on his desk.

"I didn't know Charming had a new doctor. I know just about everyone here, and I've never heard of you before, Dr. Kramer."

"That's because I just got called in for Cal's case. It seems I'm the only psychiatrist that both the defendant and the prosecuting attorneys could agree on to evaluate and hypnotize Cal."

"Ah. So you've done this kind of thing before? I was worried they hired just anyone to implant the idea in Cal's head that he had been abducted by aliens."

He looked at me and then barked out a laugh. He shook

his head. "That's funny. You have quite the sense of humor, Mrs. Jones."

"You have to, in order to make it through this world, Dr. Kramer."

I sat there, waiting for the doctor to say something.

"So, how do you think I can help Cal in his case?"

He gave me a very slight smile and then leaned back in the chair, arms folded across his stomach.

"Come now, Mrs. Jones. I think we both know you are more involved with this case than anyone else in Charming."

"Me? What would I know about a guy killing his mistress?"

He stood and walked around his desk, then grabbed a manuscript off the bookshelf and sat back down. The book was old, the leather hardened with age, the pages yellowed by time. He looked at the book and then at me. "You're what, Mrs. Jones? Thirty-two?"

"Thirty-five."

His eyes widened. "How astonishing. You don't look a day over twenty-eight."

"How very nice of you to say that. I'll give my compliments to the doctor who does my Botox," I said, trying to remain polite. "That book looks very old. What is it? A volume on hypnosis?"

"No. This is not just any book." He opened the tome and spread the book out on the desk. Then, very slowly, he slid the book over to me and tapped his finger on a specific paragraph.

"It's a book on legend and mythology."

"Really?" I took the cup of tea and raised it to my lips, taking another sip and letting the hot liquid slide down my throat. I looked at him. His gaze was tracked on my hand clutching the teacup. I gently set the cup down and looked at the book.

"How very interesting. What kinds of creatures? Fairies and goblins?"

"No, werewolves and vampires."

My stomach clenched.

I could feel his gaze stick to me as I looked at the pages. He was waiting for a reaction.

I trained my gaze on the page in question and looked at the words, trying to make sense of them. I had to brace myself to remain stoic at what the words said.

Vampires and other mythical creatures in American history.

I tried so very hard to keep my shock from showing.

"Dr. Kramer, I'm not sure I understand what this is about or what werewolves have to do with Cal. Surely, you don't think he's a werewolf, do you?" I gave him my best serious expression.

He chuckled. "Of course not, Mrs. Jones. I don't believe Cal would make a very good werewolf. He's too weak."

"Odd choice of words."

"Oh, Mrs. Jones. Let's just be honest with each other. Just because I'm a doctor and believe science, doesn't mean I don't believe in the paranormal, too."

Fear began to close my throat. I didn't want to be sitting here, having this conversation.

I glanced at the watch on my wrist and gave him a bored look. "Dr. Kramer, can you kindly get to the point? I don't have time for this nonsense."

"Fine. Very well. I appreciate your directness, so I will *get to the point* as you say.

"Cal had a memory of you the night of the murder. In fact, I have evidence that Cal had two memories of you. One, the night of the murder, and another *after* the murder. But I'm not so sure what to believe and what not to believe. So, tell me, Mrs. Jones, did you see Cal the night of the murder?"

"No. I was with my ex-husband that night. You see, it was

his birthday, and I had a surprise for him."

"So, you didn't see Cal at all that night?"

"Like I said, it was the day of my ex-husband's birthday. And it snowed that night. No one could drive in that. Especially here in Mississippi."

"Okay. So how do you explain him bringing up your name when I asked him about the murder during hypnosis? He kept saying your name and mentioning blood. Why in the world would he even say that?"

My stomach clenched and roiled with nausea. But I maintained my pleasant mask. "To be honest, hypnosis has always had a bad reputation. Who knows what Cal was talking about. I mean, hypnosis isn't exactly reliable."

"You're talking about alien abductions, right?" He pushed his chair away from the desk and glared at me hard. "Mrs. Jones, this is very serious. And I will do whatever it takes to get my client off the hook."

"Even if he committed the murder?" I knew Cal had murdered that poor girl.

He crossed his hands over his stomach and looked at me. "I'll do whatever it takes. Especially when I have some evidence that he was compelled to do it for someone else."

He flipped some pages in the book. He stopped at a page and tapped his fingers on an illustration. "People can be compelled by powerful creatures to do the unthinkable."

I looked at the drawing. It was a picture of a male vampire biting a human. His fangs were dripping with blood, and his eyes were red.

Terror welled up inside me. I wasn't sure what to do. Dr. Kramer knew I was a vampire, or at least he suspected I was. I wasn't so sure how I was going to get out of this one.

"Before you say anything, I'm just going to let you know... I'm going to do whatever it takes to prove to the world who and what you are."

CHAPTER 7

*A*fter Dr. Kramer had confronted me with his suspicions about who I was, he promptly left the room. As soon as he left, I gathered my things and walked to my car. I had no idea what to do next. I was scared. I was tired. More importantly, I wanted to talk to Khalan.

But I knew he would be unavailable until the sun went down.

So, I went home and lay in bed until I finally fell asleep.

That night when I woke up, fear settled in my gut again.

I went to the bathroom and sat in front of the mirror, closing my eyes tight and concentrating on Khalan. I knew he could feel my emotions and would know I needed him.

The doorbell rang.

I raced to the door, still dressed in yoga pants and a cami.

"Hey, girl. Hope you don't mind me dropping by." Gina smiled broadly.

She walked inside before I could say a word. I scanned the yard to see if Khalan was out there hiding behind a tree. He wasn't.

I shut the door and followed her into the living room.

She eased onto the couch.

"I wasn't expecting you. Would you like some wine?"

"No. I am training for a new marathon, and I'm trying to lose a couple of pounds. But I would love some hot tea."

"Sure." I headed into the kitchen and grabbed a couple of green teas and stuffed the bags into two coffee mugs. I turned on the electric tea kettle. In less than a minute, the water began to boil. I poured the hot water over the teabags and carried the mugs into the living room.

I handed one to Gina and laughed. "Girl, the only way you are losing weight is if you cut off your arm. You are thin as a rail already."

"That's what my husband says." She glanced at her watch on her wrist and nodded. "Good thing I walked over. Got my steps for the day."

I eased onto the couch beside her and took a sip of the tea. "So, what's up?"

Gina sat her coffee cup on the side table and pulled a couple of papers out of her purse, along with a pen.

"I brought the application for the charity dating event. I wanted to make sure you got in. The competition is going to be stiff. So, I'm going to help you fill out your paperwork."

I pressed my fingers to my lips. "I completely forgot about that, Gina. I have a lot going on."

"Of course. That's why I'm here to make sure you fill it out." She gave me the side-eye. "And that's why I am going to help you fluff up the application. You don't want to seem desperate, do you?"

"How am I going to seem desperate? I'm not really sure I want to do this dating thing at all, let alone beg for some guy's attention."

"Ha. I knew you would try to weasel out of this." Gina clicked her pen. "Let's start with the basics." Gina gave me a hard look. I filled out your name and your age. We're going to have to take a picture to go along with the application."

"A picture for what? It's not a beauty contest, is it?"

"No, of course not, but it helps to have a picture. For the application process. Once you're accepted, they'll need a picture anyway. Who knows? You might find your soulmate."

"I don't know, Gina. I don't think I have a soulmate." I threw my head back on the couch and stared up at the ceiling.

"Look. I know you're having a hard time with Miles dating and all of that crap. I'm not telling you to marry these guys. All I'm saying is go out and take a chance. What's the harm in that?"

It would probably take my mind off the stuff with Cal, if nothing else.

"Fine. What do I need to fill out?"

Gina clapped her hands together and squealed. "Oh, this is going to be so much fun."

For the next thirty minutes, I was held prisoner while Gina asked me questions, filled out the form, and gave me a slim chance at finding a little bit of happiness.

"*W*hat is this?" Khalan shoved a piece of paper in my face. He'd let himself in while I was relaxing in the bathtub.

"Will you please step out until I get dressed?" I scowled. I had attempted to cover myself with a nearby towel, and now it was sopping wet.

"Answer me." He narrowed his eyes.

I looked at the paper in his hand. "Oh, that must be the charity dating thing that Gina made me fill out." My eyes widened. "It's not all over the website, is it?"

"It is. There's a whole list of who's attending this desperate fiasco, and you were the first female listed on the Aces and Eights Dating for Charity site."

"Aces and Eights. That's catchy." I sighed. "I hope they're not expecting me to spend a whole lot of money on this shindig."

I wasn't hurting for money. In fact, I'd made out like a bandit in the divorce. And I had a good-paying job as a photographer. But I wasn't one to waste money, either. Especially now that I was supporting myself and my girls. Besides,

I wasn't sure there was a retirement plan for vampires. I had to save money where I could.

"You cannot be serious." He glared.

"What? I did it because Gina asked me to. It's for charity. It's not like it's a serious dating thing."

He threw his head back and laughed. "You couldn't be more right. This whole thing is a joke." He headed for the door. He grabbed a towel out of the bathroom closet and then threw it at me.

I caught it in mid-air.

"Wait, what do you mean? A joke?" Once he was out of sight, I scrambled out of the bathtub and wrapped the towel around me.

I hurried out of the bathroom after him.

I found him lounging on my sofa with the remote.

"Tell me. What do you mean?" I tightened my towel and crossed my arms, waiting for a reply.

He gave me his best bored look. "About what?"

"You said the whole thing was a joke." I narrowed my eyes. "Why did you say that?"

"Because it's a bunch of divorced people who are hard-up, looking for a booty call. I saw the website. It's a bunch of old, desperate people."

I pressed my lips into a firm line and fisted my hands at my sides. "Are you calling me old?"

"You're thirty-five. Not exactly a spring chicken."

"Yeah. Well, I look pretty damn good for my age," I said.

"Well, you're a vampire."

"I think the event's a good idea." I lifted my chin. "I think it's a group of professionals who are looking for companionship."

He barked out a laugh. Khalan never laughed.

It pissed me off.

"You know, I don't really care what you think."

"I'm sure you don't. But you do care about the fact that your husband is dating."

"How did you know about that?"

"I make it my business to know everything." He gave me a look that made my stomach warm.

When we first met, I couldn't stand him. And the feeling had been mutual. Since then, we'd found ourselves in each other's arms more times than I cared to admit.

It wasn't sexual, but it was still pretty hot.

"So, I suppose you're going to forget this thing." He crossed his arms and studied me.

His gaze lingered on the tops of my breasts, his pupils dilated. It startled and pleased me at the same time.

"It's been a while since I was with someone. I feel like I need to get back out there."

He stood and walked over to me. He was only inches away from me. I uncrossed my arms and tried to regulate my breathing.

"This is a fool's errand." He growled.

"What's wrong with me wanting to go on a date? Wanting to go out to dinner? Have a stimulating conversation?"

"You already have those things," he said. "We feed on humans. I listen to you bitch about your life. We talk about the movies you watch that are stupid."

"You are such an asshole."

He turned on his heel and headed for the door.

Part of me felt disappointed that he wasn't staying. But that was Khalan.

I'd forgotten to even tell him about the meeting with the psychiatrist.

I fisted my hands and growled. Sometimes, men were so frustrating.

Especially if they were vampires.

CHAPTER 9

*T*hat night after Khalan had left, I headed over to Carla's house.

I needed to find out why she'd allowed Cal to be hypnotized and how much she really knew about me.

I knocked on the door and then rang the doorbell. I cupped my hands and peered through the windowpane.

I saw movement.

The door opened, and Carla stood there with a glazed look on her face.

"Rachel? What are you doing here?"

"Carla? Can I come inside?" I cocked my head and studied my neighbor.

"Okay." She stepped out of the way and allowed me entrance.

Carla let me in, and I looked around her living room.

My neighbor usually kept her house spotless, but since Cal had gone to jail, she'd let the house go.

"What do you need, Rachel?"

"I haven't seen you in a while. I thought I would drop by and see how you were getting along." I looked around at the stacks of magazines, newspapers, and dirty dishes. "But from the looks of things, I don't think you're doing so great."

I picked up a stack of magazines to clear a spot for me to sit on the couch.

"I'm doing okay," she said. I cleared a spot on the couch for her and motioned for her to sit.

"You don't look like you're doing well, Carla. Have you seen Cal lately?"

"I saw him last week," Carla said and placed her hands in her lap. "Rachel, I need to tell you something."

"What is it?" I leaned forward in my seat.

"Cal's attorney decided to let the psychiatrist hypnotize him." She shook her head. "Cal was so mad, they had to sedate him."

"Is that even legal?" My eyes widened. "Can they do that against his will?"

"I guess so. The lawyer said it will help Cal's case." She looked at me. "You know they think he might get the death penalty if he's found guilty."

"What?" My mouth dropped.

"Yeah. That's why they wanted to hypnotize him. Thinking he could remember some details about what happened the night of the murder."

Silence stretched between us.

"Dr. Kramer said he called you into his office." Carla looked over at me. Her expression was hard to read. She was stoic and calm. Unlike the wife of a man accused of murder, who was possibly facing the death penalty.

"He thought I might have seen Cal the night of the snow-storm." I shook my head. "But I told him I was at home. It was Miles' birthday, and it was snowing." I gave her a slight smile.

"The snowstorm. The night my life was destroyed." She looked at me.

"Carla, have you been drinking?"

"No. I took a Valium. It helps me get through the day. And it kind of blocks out all the negativity. Especially when I'm at the grocery store. Used to be I couldn't get out of the car without someone running over to me and asking me questions about Cal." She shrugged.

"You really shouldn't be driving while taking that, you know."

"Who else is going to do it?" She stood and looked out into her back yard. "You know I had to sell the RV?"

"You did?" Cal and Carla would take their RV out for three weeks every spring. They made a trip to Yellowstone every year. Carla had once told me that when Cal retired from work, they planned to go RVing full-time.

Now, her life had been turned upside down.

"I'm sorry."

"Don't be. The RV was Cal's idea. He loved camping out." She looked at me from behind the haze of the Valium. "You know he never once took me to a nice hotel with a spa? That's the kind of vacation I wanted to have. Not camping, where the bears came and tried to get into our RV, looking for food."

"That actually happened?"

"It did when Cal left the garbage outside the door."

She shook her head. "I always told him to make sure there was no food left out. Yet that man always managed to leave the garbage by the RV door. He claimed he kept forgetting to put it in the trash bin. But I knew better. He was just too lazy to walk to the nearest receptacle."

"I don't know, Carla. When I was married to Miles, he forgot stuff all the time."

She jerked her head in my direction and glared. "No. Men don't forget. Not if it's important. They forget things that aren't important or dear to them."

I had a feeling she was talking about more than just forgotten garbage.

"So, do you think you'll miss the RV? I mean, you guys took trips every single year."

"Nope. Not in the least. In fact, I'm planning a vacation right now." She tapped the side of her head. "Right in here. I have it all mapped out."

I was beginning to worry about my neighbor. I'd never seen her act so out of it. Or take anything stronger than an aspirin. I was pretty sure the first time she'd gotten drunk was at my house for book club.

"Yeah? Where do you want to go?"

"I want to go to New York City at Christmas and see everything lit up. I want to ice skate and drink hot chocolate. I want to go see a Broadway play and then eat at an expensive restaurant. I want to rent a car and then drive all the way to Vermont to a bed and breakfast and stay for a week, just reading and looking out my window at all the snow. I want to go somewhere where no one knows me or knows what my husband did. I want to start over and be someone different." She cocked her head. "Rachel, do you think I'm too old to start over again?"

"Of course not, honey. I believe you can start over at any age." I swallowed. If she only knew I was starting over at thirty-five—as a vampire.

A slight smile crossed her lips. "Good. That's good. I guess I'll have to wait until Cal's case goes to trial. Once that business is over, then I can start living again."

Unease snaked up my spine. I wasn't very comfortable at all with the way our conversation was going.

"I guess I should be going." I stood.

Carla looked up at me from her seat, her expression still glazed over. "Okay. Thanks for stopping by."

I let myself out and hurried across the street. Once I stepped inside my house, I locked the door.

She had been no help. I would have to take on Dr. Kramer on my own.

One more day in the life of a vampire.

CHAPTER 10

$\mathcal{I}$t was Friday night and well after two a.m. when I met Khalan in the parking lot downtown to go feed.

He said nothing when I slid out of my Volvo wearing black jeans, boots, and a black shirt. He only lifted an eyebrow.

"Hey."

"Hey, yourself," he said gruffly.

I rolled my eyes.

"I see you are full of words tonight. As usual," I goaded him. I didn't care. I was hungry and wasn't in the mood for his shit.

"Look, Roadkill…"

"Ah, so we are back to that, are we?" I stopped and faced him.

"Back to what?"

"Back to hating me and despising me. You can't even have a decent conversation without insulting me." I pointed at him and glared. "This is why I need to do that stupid charity dating thing. So I can have one night where I can have an adult conversation with someone who doesn't think I'm an idiot."

"I don't think you're an idiot," he said.

I crossed my arms over my chest and tapped my foot.

"What are you doing?" He narrowed his eyes.

"I'm waiting for you to take a dig at me. Insult me. Put me down. Remind me how pathetic I am. How weak I am. How..."

He stepped closer and covered my mouth with his fingertips. "I never said you were pathetic."

My lips warmed at his touch. I hated how my body reacted to him. It was like I had no control whatsoever.

I grabbed his hand and moved it away from my mouth. "Actually, you did."

"When?"

"When you first turned me."

"That doesn't count." He shrugged.

I sighed. "I don't want to talk about this right now. I have a lot bigger problems to be concerned about."

"Like what?"

"Like that stupid Dr. Kramer, who called me into his office. I'm pretty sure he thinks I'm a vampire." I shook my head and started walking. "Or one of those creatures out of that book."

"What book are you talking about?" Khalan grabbed my arm and stopped me. "And why are you just now telling me about this?"

I turned around and glared at him. I wrenched my arm free.

"Because I couldn't get ahold of you." I cocked my head. "You know, you really should get a cell phone."

"Never." He growled and then crossed his arms, waiting for me to finish the story. "Tell me what happened."

"So, Cal was indeed hypnotized. Against his will. Cal's

attorney insisted on it. He feels like it will help his case if Cal can remember what happened that night."

"A bunch of fucking fools." Khalan placed his hands on his hips. "That's totally illegal."

"See, that's what I said. But, apparently, they don't seem concerned with the law."

"So, what did the doctor say?"

"He said that when he hypnotized Cal, he kept saying my name."

"But you were nowhere near him the night of the murder. That's the night I turned you."

"That's not exactly true. I saw Cal when I was driving away from home. I was so upset after seeing Nikki and Miles in bed together that I forgot to put any clothes on. That's why I glamoured him into forgetting about the night of the snowstorm."

Khalan stared at me for a beat and then cocked his head.

"I didn't want him telling anybody that he saw me driving off half-naked in a snowstorm after midnight."

"I told you, you didn't know what you were doing when it came to glamouring a human."

"I know, I know. But you have to understand, I was desperate."

He glared.

"Anyway, Dr. Kramer pulled out this book of mythological creatures with vampires and werewolves and Fae. He said that he believes Cal was compelled to kill that girl."

Khalan took a step towards me. "He said that word? Compelled?"

"Yeah. Isn't compulsion and glamour the same thing?"

Khalan didn't answer me.

"So now, I'm not sure what to do."

"Well, if he didn't mention anything about you running around naked the night of the murder, then I'm guessing he's just trying to intimidate you into saying something. He thinks you're guilty, and if he puts enough pressure on you, you will finally crack and confess."

"Confess? But I didn't do anything." I propped my hands on my hips.

"I know that, but he doesn't. He's just trying to save his patient." He shook his head. "I'll do a little digging on the good doctor."

"And in the meantime?" I looked at him.

"In the meantime, we eat." He continued towards the tattoo shop.

The overhead door dinged when Khalan opened it, and the guy at the counter reading a comic book looked up. "Sorry, we're closed."

Kalan stepped up to the counter and leaned into the guy's personal space. He whispered something low, and when he was finished, the guy had a spot of drool at the corner of his mouth.

Khalan turned and motioned me forward with a wave of his hand. I followed him down the hallway. He opened the door that led to the alley behind the building.

It used to irritate me to go through a maze just to end up outside again. But Khalan had assured me that it was to make sure he wasn't being followed. Now that Dr. Kramer suspected I was a vampire, I didn't mind the necessary precautions.

I spotted a slim figure in the shadows.

I looked over at Khalan. "That's too small to be Blayze."

"You would be correct. Blayze and I had a come-to-Jesus moment."

"So, he no longer works here?"

"Oh, he works here. He's just not in charge anymore." Khalan gave me a rare smile. He continued walking.

"Khalan. Rachel." Jennifer smiled at us.

"Hey. I didn't expect to see you here." She'd told me how Blayze was charging a lot of money to people who wanted to be an offering for a vampire. They all thought it was part of a role-playing game for vampire fanatics. What they didn't know was that the vampires were very real. After we fed, we glamoured them into forgetting what had really happened.

"Yeah. Khalan offered me the position after he demoted Blayze." Her grin widened.

"Congratulations." I meant it. I hated to see anyone getting taken advantage of.

"Thank you so much." She opened the door. "I have someone special tonight for you both."

Khalan let me walk in first, and then he followed.

I was surprised by what I saw. The smoke from the fog machine was gone, and the red lighting had been replaced by dim, white lights. It gave the room a romantic feel. White candles sat atop the tables, along with small red roses in vases.

"It looks really good." I nodded at Jennifer.

"Thank you. I listened to Khalan's suggestions on how he wanted the place to look. When people come here, they want the authentic vampire experience, not some video game version." She headed over to the bar to speak to a young man.

"You told her to do this?" I elbowed Khalan in the side.

"I just suggested." He shrugged.

"I wasn't kidding. It looks really good. I wouldn't have pegged you for a romantic vampire with style."

"Good. 'Cause I don't have a romantic bone in my body." He growled.

"Or style," I said with a big smile.

Before he could give me a sarcastic comeback, Jennifer was walking over to us again.

"I have a booth reserved for you. Just follow me this way." She took us to a booth that was tucked into a dark corner.

She turned and waved over the young man she'd been talking to by the bar.

He was in his early twenties, wearing jeans and a hoodie. His hair was too long, but his face was beautiful, like a model. He stuck his hands into his jeans' pockets and didn't smile when he walked over to us.

"Khalan, Rachel, this is Nick."

"Hello." His gaze slid from Khalan to me.

"Hi, Nick." I offered him my hand. He blinked and then shook it.

Khalan remained silent.

"I'll leave you to your guest." Jennifer smiled and headed back to the bar.

"Ladies first." Khalan motioned for me to slide into the booth. I scooted in as far as I could, and then Nick slid in next to me. Khalan sat on the other side of him.

My heart raced with what was coming next.

Khalan looked at Nick and held his gaze. "This is all a game. When you wake up in the morning, you won't remember tonight."

Nick's eyes glazed over. He leaned his head against the back of the booth.

Khalan looked at me, indicating I should have the first bite. I licked my lips. My stomach cramped with bloodlust. I pressed my lips to Nick's neck and bit. The coppery taste filled my mouth. I sighed as I drank.

Khalan bit the other side of Nick's neck. His hand wrapped around my neck as he feasted.

Desire swept through me as his thumb made tiny circles on my skin.

I wasn't sure how long I drank, but the next voice I heard was Khalan's next to my ear.

"That's enough, Rachel." His deep voice made me hunger for something other than blood.

I pulled my head back, and I couldn't help myself. He was so close, and his breath smelled of sweet blood.

I grabbed his head with both hands and pressed my lips to his. I kissed him deeply, my tongue swirling against his. It wasn't enough.

I crawled over a lethargic Nick and straddled Khalan in the booth without breaking the kiss. I ground myself down on his erection and sucked his tongue into my mouth.

He growled, and his hands clamped down on my hips. I reached between our bodies and fiddled with the button on his jeans.

"Rachel." Khalan pulled his face away from mine.

I kissed and licked his neck.

"Rachel." His hoarse voice shot through me. I managed to get his button undone and reached for his zipper.

"Rachel!"

Suddenly, I was flying through the air. I landed hard on my back in the middle of the room. Everyone turned and stared, but no one volunteered to help me up.

I pushed myself up on my arms. Khalan was standing by the booth, his jeans buttoned and everything in place. His eyes were hard and fixed on me, a look of pure hatred on his face.

I felt my face go red with embarrassment and quickly got to my feet.

Khalan walked over to me. "You should not have done that."

"No, shit." I shoved him in the chest. He didn't even flinch. "This is what I've been telling you. This is why I need to go to that dating event. I need to find someone I can talk to. Someone that cares for me. Someone I can…"

"Fuck?" He glared.

I lifted my head. He was crass, but he wasn't wrong.

"Yeah. Someone I can fuck." I headed towards the door. When I got outside, I realized that Khalan had stayed behind.

Probably to feed on someone else. Likely some female.

I fisted my hands and hurried in the direction of my car. I was going to that charity dating event, and I was determined to find someone for me.

Even if it was just for a one-night stand.

CHAPTER 11

"*M*ommy, what are you going to wear?" Gabby looked at me as she ate her apple while I cooked dinner.

"I'm not sure, honey. Probably something out of my closet. You know I have that black dress that I like so much."

"No. Absolutely not." Arianna entered the kitchen.

I stopped stirring the sautéed onion in the skillet and turned. "I thought you liked that dress."

"I do, Mom, but this is a date. Who knows, you might find someone great there. The one you're supposed to be with forever."

"I doubt that," I mumbled, but she still heard me.

Arianna gave me a hard stare.

I shook my head. "You have a lot more confidence in this than I do." I laughed. "Honey, this is just a date. Nothing serious. Just an opportunity to meet someone single, who I can have a good conversation with, and maybe go out to dinner. I'm not looking for a soulmate."

"You say that now. But you never know. This may be your chance to fall in love again. Maybe with all these things falling into place, it means it's fate. And you may find the man of your dreams." Arianna crossed her arms and looked at me.

I tried not to laugh but failed miserably. "That's really very sweet of you to say. But I don't really believe in love at first sight."

"Yeah, me neither," Gabby said, her mouth full of apple.

I TURNED my attention back to the task at hand. I cut up the potatoes and sautéed them in the sizzling skillet of olive oil.

"What about the wizard?" Gabby sighed.

"Yeah, what about the Unabomber?" Arianna narrowed her eyes at me.

"Number one, he is not a wizard or a Unabomber. He is a gardener. And I only used him that one time to fix the flowerbed."

"I really thought he liked you. In a magical sort of way." Gabby cocked her head and studied me.

"Liked me?" My eyes widened. "What on earth gave you that idea?"

"Come on, Mom. He carried you into the bedroom." Gabby waggled her eyebrows.

"That's because I was feeling ill after..."

"After you and Dad got into an argument." Arianna finished my sentence.

"I already told you guys, I fainted because I hadn't eaten that day." The truth was that I had fainted because I'd needed to drink some blood.

"Let's get back to discussing what Mom's going to wear for her date."

"Fine." I crossed my arms over my chest. "What do you think I should wear for this charity event?"

"I think you should go to Becky's and get a new dress," Arianna said.

"I don't know. I don't really need a new dress. I have a lot of stuff in my closet to choose from."

"Mom, you gotta stop." Arianna's expression hardened.

"Stop what? What do you mean?"

"You shop for us all the time and never treat yourself, especially since the divorce. This is your one chance to get a really great dress, go have a fun time, and look beautiful." Arianna nodded.

I SMILED AT HER. "That's really sweet, honey."

"Trust me, Mom. I really think you need to do this." Arianna averted her gaze.

I could tell when my daughter was keeping something from me. It came from years and years of knowing her character.

"Arianna, why is it so important for me to buy a new dress?"

She looked at Gabby. Gabby shrugged. "You might as well tell her."

"Tell me what?"

"Apparently, you're not the only Jones that will be going to this charity dating event." Arianna held my gaze.

"What do you mean?"

"I saw Dad fill out an application for the thing." Arianna sighed.

I shook my head. "But I thought he was dating someone."

"Dad said he likes to keep his options open. Whatever that means." Gabby shrugged.

I was shocked that Miles had actually said that to our children.

He was a poor example of a parent. It was something I'd

learned to deal with over the past few months after our divorce. I'd never thought he was the kind of man who put his selfishness above setting a good example for our girls, though.

"I see."

"Mom, I wasn't going to tell you. I didn't want to upset you." Arianna's face fell.

I put my spatula down and walked over to my daughter. I pulled her into a hug.

"You don't need to apologize for anything. You didn't do anything wrong. I want you and Gabby to know that you can always talk to me. About anything."

"I know, Mom." Arianna smiled. "But I still want you to get your hair and makeup done. And I want you to walk into that event like you own it."

I nodded and kissed her cheek. Then I went over to Gabby and kissed her, too.

I returned to the stove and picked up my spatula. "I have the best children in the world." I stirred the potatoes. "I think you girls are right. I'm going to go get a dress first thing tomorrow."

CHAPTER 12

*A*fter talking with Gina, I was determined that I needed a dress that would turn heads. Something from a place fancier than Becky's. The charity event was getting some traction, and Gina had said that there were a lot of very wealthy men that had signed up. She didn't bother telling me that Miles had signed up, as well.

I figured she didn't want to tell me because she was afraid I wouldn't attend.

Before I left home, I heated up a cup of blood from the freezer. Khalan had brought me a couple of units in Tupperware in case I wanted a late-night snack.

It had a bite of frostbite to it and wasn't as good warmed up as fresh from a human.

But it would do in a pinch.

I pulled into Tara's Boutique. I had a few minutes before the store opened, so I decided to check my email.

After I'd cleared out my mailbox, I decided to Google the charity dating event.

I was surprised to see that I had to have a password to get into the actual site to see who was attending.

I narrowed my eyes. "So, how did Khalan get in?"

He was probably some kind of hacker. I wouldn't put it past the vampire.

I glanced up from my phone and noticed that the store lights were on. I grabbed my purse and headed inside.

"Well, hello, Mrs. Jones." Mrs. Jenkins, the owner of the high-end store, greeted me at the door with a kind smile. "So glad to see you again."

The last time I had been in here, I'd had an argument with Veronica. It ended with me punching a hole in the wall. I, of course, paid for the repairs, but I still felt guilty about what had happened.

"Hello, Mrs. Jenkins. I'm here because I need a dress."

She clasped her hands together and let out a squeal. "That's lovely, dear. I'm so happy to see you getting back out there after your divorce."

I cringed.

She patted my hand and nodded. "You don't need to waste any more time on that lousy ex of yours. I, for one, am glad to see you ready to put yourself out there again. Now, tell me, what is the special event? A romantic dinner? Dancing under the stars?"

I hesitated. "Not exactly."

"It wouldn't happen to be for a dating event, would it?" Her eyes sparkled mischievously.

"How do you know about that?"

"Oh, honey, Gina has been in here telling me all about it. She came and got a gorgeous champagne-colored gown for a black-tie event in New York with her husband. She started talking about the charity dating event her husband's company is partnering with and told me she would send and recommend my boutique to anyone who was attending."

"That's very generous of her. Although, I do have to say,

yours is the only boutique that I would shop in for this kind of thing. It's supposed to be very fancy."

"Oh, it is. Gina showed me the decorations for the event, so I would have some reference for how to dress my clients."

"Great. So, I guess you know what kind of dress I need."

"ABSOLUTELY. Follow me to the dressing room, and I will bring you some choices. Her gaze flitted over me for a second before meeting my eyes. "And I see you still look as slim as ever. If I didn't know any better, I would say that you were aging in reverse. You will definitely have to let me know who your plastic surgeon is."

I laughed. "I don't have a plastic surgeon. Just really good Botox," I lied.

I followed her to the back of the store where the dressing rooms were. She waved me into an empty room that had space enough for a chair, a large, full-length mirror, and a platform to stand on.

"I'll be right back with your dresses." I sat in the chair and put my purse on the floor.

I heard the little bell over the front door jingle. I figured it might be a little while since someone else had arrived.

I heard the murmur of voices, and something about the sound made the hair on the back of my neck stand up. Mrs. Jenkins walked back into my dressing room without any dresses. Her face was pale, and her eyes were wide.

"Is everything okay?" I stood and tried to look over her shoulder.

"I'm afraid not." Her voice was low.

"Oh my God, is the store being robbed?" I tried to walk around her, but she was blocking the entrance to the door. She placed her hand on my arm.

"Mrs. Jones, please, I don't think you should go out there."

I looked at her. "Why not?"

She pressed her lips into a thin line, refusing to answer me.

There could only be one person that would elicit that kind of response from her. It had to be Veronica.

"I am not afraid of Veronica. This time, I promise not to put a hole in your wall." I patted her hand and walked around her.

"But that's not who it—"

I made it three feet out the door before I came face-to-face with the woman who had destroyed my family.

"Rachel? What are you doing here?" Nikki's eyes widened, and she went pale.

"What I'm doing here is none of your business. Like anything else that pertains to me." I spat the words out through clenched teeth.

"That's not what I meant." Nikki looked around, unsure of herself. It was a look I had never seen on her before.

From the moment we had become best friends, Nikki had always been there for me. In some ways, she was my polar opposite. She was shorter than me, had blond hair, and soft, brown eyes. I was tall, had dark hair, and blue eyes.

When we were friends, I'd thought she was beautiful. Now that I saw her for who she truly was, she looked like a monster.

"I'm not here to start trouble, Rachel. I just need a dress."

If that bitch told me she had a date with Miles, I was going to punch her in the face.

In our former lives, when we were best friends and told each other everything, it would've been fun to be here with Nikki, sharing this experience of getting new dresses and doing a dating event. But those days were long gone.

"You didn't tell me you were working for Uncle Stan." Nikki studied me.

"You didn't tell me you were fucking my husband," I blurted out.

"Rachel, I'm sorry. I never meant for any of that to happen. I didn't mean to hurt anyone. It just…happened."

"You made the decision to cheat. You were not satisfied with what you had at home, and you decided you wanted my husband instead. And now, Miles and I are divorced, and your husband is dead."

She narrowed her eyes at me for a fraction of a second. "How do you know that for sure?"

I rolled my eyes for dramatic effect. "It's all over town that Brad left you a suicide note. You know how small towns are. You can't keep anything hidden. I would think you would know that better than anybody."

She lowered her gaze to the floor.

"So, what are you doing here, Nikki?" I crossed my arms over my chest and glared at her. I wished my vampiric powers included shooting fire from my eyes. Because if they did, that bitch would be dead on the spot.

"As I said, I'm getting a dress. I haven't been shopping in a while, and I thought I would treat myself." She looked away when she spoke. I knew she was lying, but frankly, I didn't care.

"Mrs. Jones, I've put some lovely gowns in your dressing room." Mrs. Jenkins worried her hands and looked between us.

I was pretty sure she was wondering how much property damage she'd have on her hands.

Nikki nodded her head. "You know what, Mrs. Jenkins, I'll come back at a later time."

Nikki hurried out the front door.

Mrs. Jenkins looked at me and pressed her hands together. "I hope she didn't upset you, Mrs. Jones."

"I'm stronger than that." Though I didn't like the fact that she knew where I worked. Even Miles didn't know I was working for a private investigator.

Mrs. Jenkins smiled and nodded her head. "Yes, you are, my dear. Now, if you'll follow me, I have chosen three magnificent dresses that will look beautiful on you."

CHAPTER 13

I didn't decide on a dress. I had been too upset to even really like any of them, even though they were all beautiful. They just didn't feel right.

After leaving Tara's, I went home and slept before getting up in time to pick up the girls from school.

Since my divorce, I'd noticed that Veronica was steering clear of me. Although I was relieved, it still made me wonder.

That day, on the drive home, the girls were quiet. I was still drowsy from the sun and really wanted some blood to boost my energy.

"Mommy, what did you do all day?" Gabby asked from the back seat.

I looked at her in the rearview mirror.

"What do you mean? I'm a housewife…I mean, I'm a stay-at-home mom." It was odd that I still considered myself a housewife. It had been so embedded in my identity.

"Why are you asking such a stupid question?" Arianna shook her head.

"It's not stupid. I was wondering because we watched a

video that talked about how the parents' careers shape what the kids want to do."

"What class was that in?" I turned into our subdivision.

"History. But we had a substitute, and she made us watch a video because she didn't want to teach." Gabby shrugged. "I told the sub that I didn't agree with the video. I said that my dad's a doctor, and I have no desire whatsoever to go to medical school."

"Good, because you probably couldn't get in anyway," Arianna snarked.

"Who are you to talk?" Gabby glared. "We both know I'm smarter than you in every class. You're the one who couldn't get into medical school. You couldn't even pass the MCAT." Gabby snorted.

"What's the MCAT?" Arianna looked at her little sister.

"I rest my case." Gabby folded her arms over her chest and lifted her chin in the air.

"Girls, please. You shouldn't fight," I said.

"We're sisters. We will fight until the day we die. It's natural. And it's in the Bible. Like Cain and Abel." Gabby smiled.

I gave her a stern look.

"She's right, Mom," Arianna agreed. "If we didn't fight, we would be dead."

"Stop talking about all that stuff." I turned into our driveway and pulled into the garage.

"What? Death? It's part of life." Arianna sighed.

"She's right," Gabby agreed.

"Well, I don't like you guys talking about all that morbid stuff." I killed the engine and opened my door.

Both girls scrambled out of the car.

"Don't worry, Mom." Arianna looked over her shoulder. "I'm sure you'll live a very long life. Heck, you might even outlive us." She disappeared into the house.

A shiver ran down my back. I pressed the button for the garage door. I stood in the corner, watching until the door met the concrete and blocked out the sunlight. There was comfort in the dark.

I wrapped my arms around my chest.

I hadn't thought much about death, not mine, at least since I was a vampire now. But my girls were not. They weren't invincible or immortal.

They were human and fragile and limited.

Tears stung the backs of my eyes, and I wiped away a stray drop. I didn't want them to see me cry. I always tried to be strong, at least in front of them. I didn't want them growing up being afraid of the world. I wanted them to feel safe and happy and loved.

It hit me then that there would come a time when they wouldn't be here on this Earth. But I would be.

A wave of sorrow washed over me so strong that it brought me to my knees.

"What are you doing?" Gabby looked at me from the kitchen door.

"I dropped my purse, and everything spilled out. I'll be right in."

Once Gabby went inside, I stood and composed myself. I took several deep breaths. I had to stop thinking beyond one day at a time. Right now, I had my children. And who knew? Despite me being a vampire, I could get my head chopped off and die.

I sighed and walked into the house.

CHAPTER 14

"*R*achel, where have you been? I've been trying to call you all evening."

Uncle Stan did not sound happy.

"Sorry, my phone died, and I forgot to plug it in. What's going on? Is something wrong?"

"I ended up hiring a freelancer to track down Brad Stollings."

Nausea rolled around in my stomach. This wasn't good.

"So, you hired out instead of using one of your own private investigators?"

"Yeah, it seems this is going to be more complicated than I first thought." His voice was hoarse. I could tell he wasn't happy having to resort to someone outside his company.

"How's that going?"

"Actually, he's got a lead. First one I've had since I took the case. After some poking around, it seems he found some video evidence of Brad driving his truck down I-55. Apparently, he stopped at a gas station, and his truck was caught on the security video."

Bile entered the back of my throat. "Video?"

Holy shit. "Did they see Brad get out of the truck?" I knew it was impossible. I knew it because Khalan had ripped his throat out and killed him when Brad shot me in the head.

"That's the thing. The truck pulled into the gas station, but nobody got out to fill up the tank. And nobody got out to go inside either. It's very odd."

"Maybe he was just stopping at the gas station, trying to decide if he was going to go through with the suicide or not."

"Nope, that's not my theory," Stan stated.

"Why not? I mean, it makes sense to me," I prodded. I needed to get ahead of this so I could inform Khalan what was up.

"Rachel, when you've been in this business as long as I have, you learn a few things about human nature."

"So, what's your theory?"

"I'm not ready to state my theory just yet."

"So, you just called to let me know that somebody spotted Brad's truck?"

"No. I'm calling you because I want you to head up that direction yourself."

"Me? I told you before, I'm not an investigator, I'm a photographer. Remember, I'm the one that takes the incriminating pictures of cheating husbands and dirty city councilmen and people who commit insurance fraud."

"True," Stan said. "But you have something the other investigator doesn't have."

"And what's that?"

"A vehicle. Seems as if he wrecked his truck at a mud rally. And I'm not paying for a vehicle for him to drive. Your job is to drive him around tomorrow."

"That's not part of my job description."

"It is if you want to keep this job. I had two people come

in here today with their applications. One is a professional photographer."

I curled my fingers into fists. I didn't like being blackmailed like this. But I needed this job. It was more than just needing the job, though. I *wanted* this job. For the first time in my life, I had an occupation outside the house. It was something I could do at night while the girls slept, and I had a babysitter. It was very interesting, and I was good at it. Plus, people didn't normally associate me with working for a private investigator, trying to get some incriminating photos of whatever it was they were not supposed to be doing. For me, it was a perfect match.

"So, what am I supposed to do with my girls?"

"Oh, I don't mean for you to do this at night. You still have your photography job...for now.

I want you to do this after you take the girls to school in the morning. You should be back in time to pick them up," Stan said.

"Stan, I don't think tomorrow works for me I have..."

"I'm going to pay you for your time. I don't expect you to do this for free."

I really did not have a choice. I was going to have to get some blood before staying up all day tomorrow. The fresher, the better.

"Fine. What time do I pick the guy up? And where is he staying?"

"He's going to meet you at Merrill's gas station around eight-fifteen. That should give you time to drop the girls off and get on over there."

"How do I know who he is?"

"Oh, you'll know him. He'll be the one with the really good looks. The only one women will be looking at." Stan ended the call without a goodbye.

I needed blood. Otherwise, I would be falling asleep at the wheel.

"What's up?" Arianna came into the kitchen. "You look stressed."

"I need to run out for a bit. I was trying to think who to call to stay with you guys."

"Really, Mom? You do realize I'm old enough to stay by myself. Me and Gabby aren't babies anymore."

"I don't know, Arianna…" I bit my lip.

"It's not like you're going to be out all night, are you?" She cocked her head.

"No. I just have to run and pick something up." I nodded. "You're right. I think you two can stay without a babysitter."

Arianna gave me a big smile.

"I'll talk to Gabby and tell her you are in charge."

She rubbed her hands together gleefully.

"Try not to fight," I warned.

"I'll try." She hurried out of the room.

One problem solved. Now, I just had to find some blood.

CHAPTER 15

I parked my Volvo off Main Street. It was around nine, and the parking lot was full. I got out of my car and rubbed my palms on my jeans. I didn't even know if the role-play room was open. But I had to try. I needed blood.

I headed in the direction of the tattoo shop. I shoved my black Fedora on my head. I didn't want to run into anyone I knew.

I reached the shop and walked inside. The same guy was manning the desk and reading a comic with a mermaid on the front cover.

"Mrs. Jones, what are you doing here?"

I froze.

My gaze locked on Ricky Spencer. He was my next-door neighbor's son and owned a sports car, which he drove way too fast.

His parents were overindulgent and let him get away with a lot of shit.

Not only that, but he was too good-looking for his own

good. I worried whenever I caught him looking at my Arianna.

I had hoped he was going to an out-of-state college next year. But to my disappointment, he got in at Ole Miss. Which meant, he would be home every weekend.

"Ricky, what are you doing here? Aren't you a little too young to be getting a tattoo? You're not even eighteen yet."

"Are you kidding me? This is my third one." He smirked.

"Do your parents know you're here?" I glared.

"Of course, they do. They had to sign the parental consent form. Hey, take a look at this beauty." He pulled up the front of his shirt, revealing a fresh tattoo. It was a snake that wrapped around his belly button with the word *badass* on the snake's head.

"That looks like it hurt."

"Not as much as the tattoo on my spine. It's a Komodo dragon. That hurt like a bitch." He grinned and let his gaze drift down to my breasts.

"So, tell me why you're here, Mrs. Jones. Getting a new tattoo since your husband left you?"

I forced myself not to throat punch him. "Let's get something straight. My husband did not leave me. I threw his ass out."

He ran his hand across his crotch and adjusted himself. "Must get very lonely over there in that big house all by yourself. You know, I'm free anytime you need somebody to give you some...company." He winked.

The guy behind the desk looked up and studied our exchange with interest. His comic book was quickly forgotten.

I knew there was no way I would be able to sneak into the role-playing building without Ricky following me.

"I have to go." I turned on my heel and headed towards my car. My shoes clicked as I hurried down the sidewalk.

Tomorrow was going to be a long day. It was going to suck since I hadn't gotten to feed.

I made it back to my car and unlocked the door. The parking lot had thinned out considerably.

My stomach rumbled. I pressed my hand against my abdomen.

"Hey, Mrs. Jones! Wait up." Ricky hurried towards me.

I WANTED to get in the car and drive away from the asshole, but I didn't.

I was sure before dawn broke, he would tell the whole neighborhood that he'd seen me at the tattoo place, shopping for new ink.

"What do you want, Ricky?" I sighed.

He waited until he was a few feet from me and then grinned. "I want some money."

"What?" I must have heard him wrong.

"Money. I want some money." He lifted his head.

"Money. You want money from me?" I broke out into laughter. When I was done, I shook my head. "Yeah. That's not going to happen."

"Everyone knows you wiped your husband out in the divorce. At least that's what Mom said. Good job, by the way." He playfully punched me on the shoulder and grinned.

"Ricky, you have money for a tattoo and gas for that expensive car. If you need cash, you should learn to budget better. If you need funds, then you should get a job.'"

"Job? No way." He wrinkled up his nose. "I don't have time for a job."

"Right." Ignoring him, I hit the unlock button on my key fob. "Then just ask your parents for more."

"I can't do that. They said they were going to start limiting how much they give me. Said they were saving it for college." He crossed his arms and scowled. "Parents blow. They don't understand I have needs."

"Like the need for a new tattoo?" I was exhausted from this conversation.

"Exactly." He nodded.

"Yeah, I'm not giving you money, Ricky."

"Really? Well, I would hate for the whole neighborhood to find out you were getting a tattoo because you're so depressed about your divorce. Why, the next thing you'll be doing is fucking a young guy. Like me."

I narrowed my eyes on him. I'd never wanted to hit somebody so much in my life. "You would not dare tell such a lie."

He snorted. "Apparently, you don't know me very well. What I want, I always get."

"Let me tell you something, Ricky Spencer, no one will believe you."

"Oh, I think they will. Hot new divorced mom with no one in her bed? I think the good people of Charming will definitely believe me."

"So you would lie about me because you want money?"

"Pretty much."

My stomach rumbled, reminding me how hungry I was for blood.

Ricky had me between a rock and a hard place.

My gaze landed on the thick vein in his neck. It throbbed with each heartbeat.

The first time I had glamoured somebody, he'd turned out to be a murderer.

Since then, I'd had a lot more practice with Khalan as my teacher. I had gotten a lot better.

"Fine. But you have to get in the car. I'm not giving you money out here in the open."

"Perfect. I would prefer our transaction to be a little more intimate." He waggled his eyebrows.

"I'm not that desperate," I gritted out.

"Maybe not now, but one day, you'll be calling me up with a need to fill that void your husband left."

I opened the front door of my car and slid in. Ricky walked around and got in on the passenger side.

Within the close confines of the car, I could smell the blood from his tattoo. My mouth watered.

I stared straight ahead. My stomach rumbled again. "How much money do you want?" I was curious. There was no way I was giving him shit.

"How about...five hundred?"

I jerked my hand in his direction. "Are you fucking crazy?"

"I got to get the snake tatt colored in. And I need some upgrades for my car." He shrugged.

The vein in his neck pulsed with each heartbeat. I leaned over the console and met his gaze.

"Ricky, I want you to listen to me very carefully."

His eyes glazed over. I could tell he was under my glamour.

"Do you understand?"

"Yes, I understand. I will listen to everything you say."

"Give me your neck," I commanded.

He laid his head back against the headrest and showed me his neck.

I glanced around the parking lot. Empty.

My mouth watered. I pressed my mouth to his flesh and bit down. Warm, coppery blood spilled into my mouth. My stomach cramped.

I opened my eyes as his heartbeat began to slow. I knew it was time to stop feeding.

I PULLED my teeth away and licked the wound. The puncture marks stopped bleeding.

I stared at Ricky. His eyes were still glazed.

"Ricky, you will not remember being bitten tonight. The last thing you remember is getting your snake tattoo and then going straight home. You never saw me. You are never going to ask anybody for money again.

"You're going to walk back to your car and go straight home. Do you understand?"

"Yes." He opened the door and got out. I watched as he made his way to his car.

I pulled down my visor and looked in the mirror. I carefully wiped the drops of blood from the corners of my mouth.

I took a deep breath and then let it out slowly.

Now that I'd had fresh blood, I could concentrate on driving that investigator around tomorrow without incident.

CHAPTER 16

I dropped the girls off at school the next morning and headed over to the gas station where I was to pick up the investigator for Uncle Stan.

It was a good thing that I'd had fresh blood the night before. Otherwise, I would be wilting under the sun.

I pulled into the gas station parking lot and killed the engine. I glanced around, trying to see if I could figure out who I was driving around all day.

It really irritated me that Uncle Stan had told me to do this. But he was my boss, and I wanted to keep my job as a photographer, so I really had no other choice.

I scanned the parking lot and the cars at the gas pumps. Uncle Stan had said the guy would stand out, and that I would know exactly who it was when I saw him. But none of the people here in Charming, Mississippi stood out. At least, not to me. I peeked at the time on my dash.

I glanced up at the front door of the gas station. Two women had stopped on their way out and were staring at something.

I looked around, trying to see what they were looking at. And that's when I spotted him.

Holy crap. It couldn't be him. Surely, not.

He spotted me, smiled, and headed straight for my car.

He opened the passenger side door and slid in without an invitation.

"Um, what are you doing here?"

"I was told that you were going to drive me around today."

"*You* are the private investigator?"

He grinned. My stomach warmed. I could not believe that Jack, the werewolf, was sitting in my car.

"I'm more of a tracker than a private investigator. Although, to humans, private investigator sounds better than tracker."

I had met Jack a few months ago when I went to check on a couple of abandoned coyote pups that had been adopted by a werewolf Pack. Khalan had been furious that I had met Jack. I didn't think it was because he was a werewolf, I imagined it was because he was a *hot* werewolf.

"So, what exactly happened to your car that I'm driving you around?"

"It's not a car, it's a truck, and I wrecked it at the mud races." He shrugged. "I seem to go through a couple of trucks a year."

"Two vehicles a year?" Maybe Khalan was right about this guy. He'd said that Jack did not belong to any of the werewolf Packs in Mississippi. He'd said that Jack was only traveling through and did not have a Pack to call his own. Jack was a loner.

"So, where exactly am I supposed to be taking you today?"

"I tracked the last sighting of Brad Stollings to a gas station. According to the video, he was driving north, so I think we should head that way towards Memphis."

"As long as I'm back before I have to pick up my girls."

"Are your girls as beautiful as their mother?" He gave me one of those looks. My heart sped up.

This whole thing was a bad idea. But it was nice to have some male attention after my divorce. And I certainly wasn't getting a whole lot of that from my Maker, Khalan. Except for the few times we had groped each other.

"WE SHOULD CHECK out the gas station and talk to anybody there who might have seen him, even though, from the video, he didn't go inside. But it was late at night, and maybe the attendant who was working that night will be here today. Or at least we can get a contact number for him."

"Sounds good." I put the car into reverse and backed out. I pulled onto the street and headed towards the highway.

"I assume you're not from Mississippi?" I glanced over at him.

He gave me a slow, easy smile, the kind that made women's hearts beat faster, and their panties drop to the floor.

"You can say I travel around a bit. Don't really have a home."

"So, where were you born?"

"I was actually born in Arkansas."

"Really? So, is that where your Pack is from? Arkansas?"

"Yes. But I haven't been back to that state in a while. I seem to do better away from my family. They're not much on affection, if you know what I mean."

"I'm sorry to hear that. I think all families have their crap they have to deal with. Some more so than others."

Jack turned in his seat. He rested a muscled arm against the back of my headrest.

"I understand you're divorced."

I looked at him and nodded. "Yes, recently divorced. I'm guessing you found that out from Uncle Stan."

"No, some guy at the bar downtown told me, actually. I was asking about you. He gave me all the information."

I cringed. "I bet he did. Everybody in Charming seems to know what happened between my ex and me."

"He must be some kind of idiot for cheating on you. With your best friend no less." His thumb dipped down and rested on my shoulder. He was unusually hot. I wondered if it was because I was a vampire, or if it was because he was a werewolf and they normally ran hot. It was just one more question I would have to ask my Maker.

"You mean my ex-best friend. I didn't only lose my husband, I also lost my best friend." I pulled onto the ramp for the highway.

"You're a free woman now, right?"

"I'm not seeing anybody, if that's what you're asking."

"So, once we get this case figured out and either find Brad Stollings alive or discover his body, maybe we can have a drink."

I didn't know if it was all the flirting he was doing or his werewolf scent, or the fact that I had not been with a man in months, but I almost agreed to the date right then.

I swallowed hard and tightened my grip on the steering wheel. "Well, you know, I'm usually busy at night with my girls, so going out isn't really in the cards for me right now. "

"But didn't you sign up for that charity dating event?" He leaned in closer. I inhaled his wonderful masculine scent. I should have drunk more blood, I needed it to resist the effect he was having on me.

"You saw it on the website. I let my friend, Gina, who is hosting, talk me into it. Plus, it's for charity." I tried to take slow, deep breaths. I had a feeling that Jack was the kind of werewolf that wouldn't take no for an answer.

"That event looks kind of fancy. Have you found a dress?" His thumb made tiny circles on my shoulder. I tried to regulate my breathing and concentrate on the road, but it was difficult.

"Not yet. I tried on a few a couple of days ago, but I wasn't really in the mood. I couldn't really find what I wanted."

"Well, I bet you would look stunning in red. You know, the color of blood."

I jerked my gaze over to him. He grinned.

"Yes, Rachel Jones, I know exactly who and *what* you are. I may be a werewolf, but I knew from the minute we met that you weren't human. I saw you hanging out with Khalan a couple of nights ago, and that's when I figured out what you were." He sat back in his seat and stared at me.

"You think you have me figured out?" I snorted.

"No. I'm still trying to figure out how a vampire is out during the day. Although I do know that the thing about your species burning up in the sun is just a myth. I was surprised, however, when Stan said that you would be driving me around today. You must have fed recently in order to stay awake during the day."

I said nothing, just stared at him. It was one thing to talk freely with Khalan about being a vampire, because he was one, too. But to talk about it with someone else made me very uneasy.

"Relax, sweetheart. I'm not telling anybody your secret. As long as you don't tell them mine." He winked.

"Why would I tell anybody you're a werewolf?" I shook my head slightly. "Nobody would believe me anyway. They would think I was crazy."

He leaned back in the seat and studied me. "You would be very surprised how many people *would* believe you. Even here in Charming, Mississippi."

I looked at him "Are you saying there are more like us?"

"What I'm saying is that some humans pose a very big threat to our kind. And the less people who know about us, the better."

"So, did you know Khalan?"

He folded his arms across his chest and stayed silent as he looked straight ahead at the interstate.

We drove in silence for what seemed like an eternity.

"Turn here. At this exit." Jack pointed ahead.

I took the exit and made a right, pulling into the parking lot of the gas station. I put the car in park and glanced over at him.

He gave me a sexy grin and patted my knee. "You wait here while I go inside."

I grabbed my phone and looked at the missed messages from Gina. She was still concerned that I hadn't gotten a dress for the dating event yet. I sent her a quick text telling her that I would get it done within a few days, and for her not to worry.

Jack walked out of the gas station, and all the women's heads turned. I couldn't blame them. He was probably the most handsome man I had ever seen. I mean, the most handsome *werewolf* I had ever seen. I didn't know the dating requirements between species. Did vampires even date werewolves? Or was that against the rules? Just one more thing I would have to ask Khalan when I saw him next.

CHAPTER 17

J laid my head back and closed my eyes. Drowsiness started to creep over me.

"You know what would make you feel more awake?" Jack slid into the passenger's seat.

"A bed?" I cracked open one eye.

"That, and my blood." He gave me a devilish grin.

I opened my eyes and cocked my head. "Is that even possible? I mean, in all the movies, vampires and werewolves hate each other."

"That's what our history has been." Once again, he rested his arm on my seat, and his fingers brushed up against my shoulder.

A shiver ran through my body.

"But you and I could change all that. Nothing like two very sexual people giving in to their pleasures." His pupils dilated, and his eyes shifted into a strange yellow color.

"I don't think that's a good idea." I shook my head, dissolving the images of him naked and on top of me as we had hot sex.

"Why not?" He grinned and leaned closer.

"Because we are here to do a job. Besides, I was warned about you." I started the engine.

"Khalan. I knew that fucker would be all up in my business." His eyes shifted back to their usual color.

"Why don't you like Khalan?"

"Let's just say we have history." Jack shrugged.

I wanted to know what kind of history. I wanted to know why his eyes had turned yellow.

"So, did you find out anything?"

"Yeah. I talked to the clerk, who happened to be here the night that Brad's truck was caught on video. He said he remembered the truck because the driver's side window was broken and it had plastic taped onto it."

My gut clenched. It was broken because Khalan had shattered it when he pulled Brad out of the car and ripped out his throat.

"So, where to next?" I yawned behind my hand.

"We are going to head to Memphis."

"Memphis? I can't spend all day in Memphis."

"Relax, sweetheart. It's only a forty-five-minute drive, and I promise to have you back before your girls get out of school."

"I was kind of hoping to get in a quick nap before." I sighed.

"We could always drive over to the motel across the street, and I can show you what you are missing." He leaned towards me.

"Easy." I pressed my hand against his very defined chest. He growled low and deep, and his eyes once again shifted to yellow.

"I can't seem to help myself around you. You make me… hard." He growled and covered my hand with his.

My eyes widened in shock and desire.

"I bet no one has ever talked dirty to you before." He grinned.

I pulled my hand away.

"I would love to show you another side of your nature."

"What do you mean?" I swallowed and looked away from the bulge in his jeans.

"As a vampire, you are more sexual than you ever were as a human."

I could smell his desire. And mine.

I licked my lips and tightened my hands on the steering wheel. "I think we need to keep this professional. I don't like the idea of getting involved with someone I'm working with."

What he'd said was true. Since being turned, I had never had so many desires. It was one of the reasons I had agreed to do the charity dating event.

"I've never met anyone like you before." He rubbed his thumb across his bottom lip.

"Of course, you have. You know Khalan. He's a vampire, too."

"That's not what I mean. You are more than just a vampire. You are...extraordinary." He let his gaze travel down my face to my chest to finally rest between my legs.

"And *you* are being rude," I snapped.

The chemistry in the car was building up, and I had to snap both of us out of it.

"My apologies. I don't mean to be. I'm just always going after what I want." A slight smile played on his lips.

"Fine." It was the best apology I was going to get from him. "Memphis, it is."

I backed out and pulled onto the ramp to get back on the interstate headed north.

*W*e didn't make it all the way to Memphis. Instead, we stopped at Southaven, Mississippi. Jack had gone in to talk to the gas station clerk while I tried to catch a quick nap. When he got back into the car, he said the clerk didn't have any information.

I was relieved. The more the lead went cold, the less chance of Khalan or my involvement with Brad's death coming to light.

"I would ask you out to lunch, but I have a feeling you don't eat what I do," Jack joked.

"You would be right." It was a little after twelve, and we were headed back to Charming. I took the exit. I relaxed as we got closer to town.

"Where do you want me to drop you off?" I glanced over at him.

"The gas station is fine."

I narrowed my eyes. "But where are you staying? Surely, they're not letting you live behind the gas station."

He laughed. "It's too far out for you to drive. But I appreciate it. Besides, I'm going to head across the street to that restaurant for a bite."

"If you're sure." I glanced over at him.

"I'm sure."

I pulled into the gas station and parked at the end of the building. I put my car in park and turned to him. "So, do you need anything else from me?"

"Yes." He moved into my space and pressed his lips to mine.

I was so shocked that I gasped. He took the opportunity and deepened the kiss. His hand cradled my neck and pulled me closer. His tongue slid against mine, and I found myself kissing him back.

Overwhelming desire washed over me, hard and fast.

I moaned against his mouth. He trailed kisses across my cheek to my neck. His hand went up my side and found the hem of my shirt.

A knock on my window had me pulling away from Jack.

I felt my face blazing bright red as I looked out my window. Fucking Veronica Counts.

"Looks like you didn't waste any time moving on after your divorce, Rachel," Veronica screeched. "Why, I thought you two were going to have sex right here in the Kum and Go parking lot."

"Who's that old bitch?" Jack narrowed his eyes.

Anger raced in my veins. I pushed the button, and the window rolled down. "Don't you have anything better to do? Like trick small children into coming to your house made of candy so you can eat them?"

The smile slid off her face like butter, and she pressed her lips into an evil line.

Jack burst out laughing. "Yeah, she kind of does look like a witch. Certainly cackles like one."

I grinned.

"For your information, my husband loves my voice. He says I have the voice of an angel."

"Yeah. A fallen one." I glared.

Ignoring my insult, she looked over at Jack. "Who's your friend, Rachel?"

"None of your business."

"He looks a little young for you. I would have figured you would have a boyfriend closer to your age. You know, around forty." She sneered.

"I don't care how old Rachel is. She has the body of a supermodel." Jack opened the door and slid out. Before he shut the door, he stuck his head in. "I'll see you tomorrow."

I watched as he walked across the street.

"Well, he didn't even offer to buy you lunch," Veronica huffed.

"Bye, Veronica." I rolled up the window, but Veronica kept talking.

I put the car in reverse and pulled out of the gas station lot.

I headed home. I needed to get a couple hours of sleep before I had to get in the car line.

I just hoped that when I closed my eyes, I didn't dream of Jack.

CHAPTER 19

That night, I was putting the dishes into the dishwasher when someone knocked on my kitchen window.

I screamed and then glared.

Khalan stared back at me.

He held up his hand and crooked his index finger at me.

I shot him the bird.

"Now," he mouthed.

"Fine," I mouthed the word back.

I started the dishwasher and headed for the back door.

"I see the Unabomber is back." Arianna walked through the kitchen to get a glass of water.

"Stop calling him that." I looked at her.

"Why don't you invite him in? It's kind of creepy that you two always go outside to talk." She cocked her head. "You're not a secret spy or something, are you?"

"No, honey. If I was, I would have known your dad was cheating."

"Touché." She nodded.

"Besides, I didn't think you liked Khalan."

"I don't know Khalan. But he's shown up for you when Dad didn't." She walked over to the back door and opened it.

"Khalan, why don't you come inside instead of lurking?" Arianna waved her hand.

Khalan looked surprised that my daughter had opened the door and not me. I was just as shocked.

Arianna sighed. "Look, I'm sorry I called you the Unabomber."

Khalan frowned. "I didn't know you did."

"Well, I said it behind your back. Not to your face. 'Cause I'm not a mean-spirited person. Like Veronica," Arianna said cheerfully.

I laughed.

Khalan looked at me.

"Come in." I waved him inside.

Khalan stepped in and, immediately, my large house seemed to shrink. It always did when he was inside.

He was dressed in his customary black trench coat, black jeans, and matching T-shirt. His biker boots thudded against my floor. His long hair was tied back in a ponytail, and his beard looked as if it had been groomed.

"Khalan, you remember Arianna." I watched the interaction between them with interest.

Arianna stuck out her hand.

I was shocked.

"Hello, Arianna." Khalan took her hand in his.

My heart flipped in my chest.

"Mommy, what's—?" Gabby stopped in her tracks when she saw Khalan. "You're here."

"I guess I am." He narrowed his eyes on her.

She smiled and walked right up to him. "You know, I like you better with your hair down and not tied back. But you still look like a wizard to me."

"Thanks. I think." He looked from my daughters to me.

"Girls, Khalan and I need to talk."

"Ugh. You never let us talk to interesting people. Like wizards," Gabby sulked.

"He's not a wizard, you idiot." Arianna frowned.

"Well, he's definitely not a Unabomber," Gabby shot back.

"So, what are you?" Arianna looked at Khalan.

"I'm the gardener."

"Ugh. I wish you people would just tell us the truth. It's not like we're little kids anymore." Arianna grabbed an Oreo out of the cookie jar and took a bite. She nodded at Gabby. "Come on, they need their privacy."

"Fine. But I want you to show me some magic tricks before you go." Gabby pointed at Khalan.

"Well, that was interesting."

"You act like I've never talked to little children before."

"It's not that. I'm more surprised that my girls were pleasant to you."

"Gabby has always accepted me." He folded his arms across his chest and leaned across the kitchen island.

"I know, but Arianna has never really been warm to you."

He nodded. "Yeah, that kind of surprised me, too."

"So, what did you need to talk to me about?"

He narrowed his eyes. "Something about you is different."

I glanced down at my shirt and jeans and then looked back at him. "What do you mean? My appearance?"

He took a step closer to me and then leaned into my space. He inhaled. When he pulled back, he glared at me.

"Who were you with today?" he demanded.

I shifted my weight and glanced at the floor. I knew this wouldn't go well for me.

"So, you know the investigator I had to drive around?"

"Yeah?"

"Well, it wasn't just some random P.I. He was a tracker."

Khalan unfolded his arms, and his eyes widened. "A werewolf."

It was more of a statement than a question.

"Yeah. And you already kind of know him."

"Jack? Are you fucking kidding me?"

He paced the kitchen, refusing to look at me.

"Yeah, it was Jack." He stopped pacing and looked at me.

I held up my hands in defense and tried to calm him down.

"I didn't know I would be driving a werewolf around all day. I thought it was just a human. And then Jack showed up and got into my car."

Khalan stopped pacing and glared at me. "He did a lot more than just ride around with you. Didn't he?"

"Why would you say that?"

"Because I can smell his scent all over you." Once again, he invaded my personal space and leaned into me, inhaling deeply.

I knew I should have taken a shower as soon as I got home.

"I didn't sleep with him, if that's what you're inferring."

"So, what *did* you do?" He didn't move but continued to invade my personal space.

My heart hammered in my chest.

"Well, he sort of kissed me."

I lifted a strand of my hair to my nose and sniffed. It didn't smell like werewolf to me.

"He rubbed his scent all over you. Can you not smell that? You positively stink like him."

I put my hands on my hips and met his gaze. "Well, I certainly didn't encourage it if that's what you mean."

"Are you sure?"

"Yeah, I'm sure."

I tried shoving him away from me, but it was like moving an oak tree.

I stormed out of the kitchen into the living room, wishing he would just leave already.

But at the thud of his biker boots, I knew that wasn't happening.

He grabbed my arm and spun me around.

"Do you know how dangerous it is for you to be involved with him?"

"Actually, I don't. Every time I ask you about him, or the werewolf species in general, you don't give me much information. So, I'm kind of out here trying to figure things out on my own."

"Vampires and werewolves hate each other. That's how it's been, and that's how it's always going to be. You have no business with him."

"So I should hate him because the rules say I should?" I arched my brow at him.

"Yeah, pretty much."

"That's the stupidest thing I've ever heard. I mean, even when we took those coyote pups to that wolf Pack, you were very respectful of them."

"There's a difference between respect and sleeping with someone."

"I did not sleep with him. He kissed me in the parking lot of the gas station. That was it. And I wished it hadn't happened."

"Oh yeah, why's that?"

"Because that bitch Veronica came knocking on my car window. The last thing I need is for her to spread more gossip about me in this town."

He walked over to the window, crossed his arms, and stared out into the back yard.

I sighed. I knew I was getting nowhere with him. It was a conversation I didn't want to have.

"So, are you curious about what we found today regarding Brad?"

"No, not really. We both know that Brad is dead. His throat was ripped out, and he, along with his truck, are buried in the Mississippi River. No one will ever find him. Not even that werewolf."

"I don't think Uncle Stan is going to give up that easily. For some reason, he has a vested interest in finding Brad alive or at least finding his body. Plus, there's a video of Brad's truck at a gas station."

Khalan turned and looked at me.

"So, are you still going through with that stupid charity dating event?"

I curled my hands into fists at my sides and glared. "As a matter of fact, I am." I didn't know how Khalan always knew how to press my buttons and infuriate me.

"What are you going to do when you meet somebody and you like him and you have to tell him you are a vampire?"

"Well, I certainly wouldn't tell him that. Besides, this isn't some kind of long-term relationship that I'm looking for. I know that my time here on Earth is going to be very long. I realize that there's no way to have a real relationship with anybody who's human. But it would be nice to get dressed up and go out on a date for a night. It will be nice to forget about what I am and what I have to look forward to for my future for a bit."

I didn't usually feel sorry for myself. It was a useless emotion. But between being kissed by Jack and harassed by Khalan, I was starting to get pretty emotional.

"You're bringing a lot of trouble on yourself by doing this. When I first turned you, I told you that you needed to leave your life behind and come with me. You have no idea how to make it in this world as a vampire on your own."

"You should realize by now that I will never leave my children. That's not something I can do." He looked at me and laughed. "Leave your children? You are pathetic. Don't you realize they are going to leave *you* one day?

"One day, they are going to get old, and they are going to get sick. And one day, they will die. Do you want to be around for that? Do you want to see your children as their lives end?"

Tears welled up and stung the backs of my eyes. I nodded. I couldn't speak around the knot in my throat.

"Don't you see that you are just prolonging the inevitable? One day, they won't be here. And one day, you'll realize that the pain of watching your children die is something you'll have to carry with you for as long as you live."

Anger and fear welled up inside of me. He was right, of course. But I didn't want to hear it.

"I think you need to leave."

He started to open his mouth to say something insulting, but then he shut it.

He walked to the back door and out into the night without another word.

As I watched him go, I realized that I had never felt more alone or afraid in my life.

*

CHAPTER 20

"*W*here's your dress?" Gina barged into the house the second I opened the front door.

"What?" It was seven o'clock on Saturday morning, and the girls were sleeping. I had planned on going to bed myself, but the damn doorbell wouldn't stop ringing.

When I opened it, Gina was standing there, looking mad as a hornet.

"Your dress. For the charity event." She turned and crossed her arms over her chest and glared.

I closed my eyes and rubbed my temple. "I haven't found anything I like yet."

She shook her head. "Don't lie. You're planning on backing out, aren't you?"

"What?" I opened my tired eyes.

"You promised me you were going to go and really give this a try. I know you, Rachel. You only told me that to get me off your back." She pressed her lips together and scowled.

I rarely saw Gina mad. At anyone. And never me.

"Gina, I promise. I will get a dress."

She cocked her head. "You know, I made sure there were

a lot of eligible bachelors in the pool for you. Men with money and ambition."

"I don't know if I want money and ambition. I think I prefer kindness and a good heart, someone who loves my kids."

Her expression softened. "I'm sorry. I didn't mean to get all up in your business like that."

"It's okay. I know you probably have a lot going on, getting the event ready."

She plopped down onto the couch and folded her hands in her lap. "I need to tell you something."

I sat next to her. "Miles is going to be there."

Her mouth dropped, and she nodded. "How did you know?"

"I saw the website."

"But you don't have the password to get in yet."

"A friend of mine does." I arched my brow.

"I'm sorry, Rachel. I didn't know Miles was going to enter until after you agreed to go. And, well, it just pissed me off that he was selfish enough to parade himself up there like that." She shook her head. "You know, he really is an asshole." She looked up at me. "I always wanted to tell you that."

"Really? I thought everyone loved Miles." My eyes widened.

"Miles is a narcissistic sociopath. He thinks of no one but himself. And his tiny dick." She cringed. "Sorry, Rachel. I just assumed he had a tiny dick."

I let out a laugh. "It's okay. You're right. He's not packing much down there."

She laughed and lifted her knees to her chin. "I just really want you to shine at the event. I want you to walk in there and make every man's head turn. And I want Miles to see what he lost."

I smiled and squeezed my friend's hand. "Thanks, Gina. I needed to hear that."

"The event is next weekend. So, you need to get your dress today," Gina implored.

"I know, I know." I sighed heavily. "It's just I've already gone to Tara's, and I ran into Nikki."

"You what?" Gina's eyes grew big. "You didn't tell me that."

"I try not to focus on the negative. Anyway, that's why I left."

"That must have been really...bad." Gina studied me.

"It could have been worse. I could have beaten her ass." I shrugged.

"I would actually like to see that." Gina grinned.

"Yeah, well, you're going to have to wait. I've got more important things to do than let Nikki take up one more thought in my head. I've got an event I need to get ready for."

"That's my girl." Gina lifted her chin and nodded slowly.

"I'll head over to Tara's and see if I overlooked something that might work."

Gina gave me a thoughtful look. "You know, Becky's is carrying a few high-end things, cocktail dresses and black-tie gowns. You should go check them out."

"That's right. The girls mentioned Becky's." I tapped my finger to my lips. "You know, when we went shopping for Easter dresses, the salesclerk showed me a dress I really liked, but it was too dressy for church."

The red number also had a hefty price tag. I ended up not getting it. But I had thought about it often since.

"Want me to come with you?"

"Sure. I just need to tell Arianna she's watching her sister while we're gone."

"You could bring them," Gina suggested.

"I have to fight Gabby to get her to go shopping, and

when Arianna finds out it's just shopping for me, I'm sure she'll want to stay home. It's just me and you."

"Perfect." Gina grinned. "It's been a while since I had some girl-time. Also, can we swing by Caffeine and Cookies so I can grab a latte?"

I cringed. "Yeah, but you probably need to go in alone. I don't want Max to see me in the drive-thru."

"Oh, yeah. Your old boss. I forgot about that. You got fired when you told some entitled college student off."

"Don't remind me. It wasn't my finest moment." I stood. "Let me just change clothes, and we will be on our way."

"Mrs. Jones, I'm so sorry we don't have that dress anymore." Hope, the salesclerk at Becky's Boutique, worried her hands.

"Really? I have been thinking about it ever since I saw it here when we were Easter shopping."

She gave me a sympathetic look. "I remember that dress on you. It was perfection. But I have some new things that we just got in that I think you might like."

I looked over at Gina, who was busy sorting through a rack of dresses.

"Hey, Rachel, what do you think about this blue gown?"

I looked at the deep blue dress she was holding. I shook my head. "No, I don't think I'll be wearing that color for a while."

"Why? The color looks perfect on you. It matches your eyes." I propped my hands on my hips and glared at her. "I think you forgot about the night at the country club. When everybody found out about Miles' affair. I was wearing that exact color dress."

"I see. But if I were you, I wouldn't let one occasion ruin a great dress."

"I know, but it's going to take a little while before I don't associate that color with the worst night of my life."

Hope came back with two dresses.

"Mrs. Jones, this green color is the latest thing. It's form-fitting and will hug you in all the right places. Plus, it has a dramatic slit up the side to show off your long legs."

I reached out and rubbed the silky material between my fingers. "This is a beautiful dress, there's no doubt about that. But I don't know about the slit. I mean, isn't that a little too racy for my age?"

Gina turned and glared at me. "Are you freaking kidding me? If I looked like you, I probably wouldn't wear clothes at all. I would just walk around naked all the time, showing everybody what a perfect body I had."

"I have children, so I can't very well run around the town of Charming completely nude."

"So, what's the other option?" The other dress was covered, so I couldn't see what was inside the bag.

Hope's eyes lit up as she held out the covered dress. She placed the green dress on a rack, and then hung up the mysterious garment bag on a hook on the wall. She slowly unzipped it and then turned to look at me.

"Now, this dress is one that no one else has seen. I just got it in this morning, and it hasn't even been out on the floor yet. So, technically, you will be the first person to see it. And there were only a small number made. It's from Paris. I don't usually bring dresses of this quality out. Only for special customers."

Gina stopped rifling through the rack and looked at me.

"Maybe this is it. Maybe this is the dress you were meant to wear to this event."

Hope gave me a grin and then turned back to the garment bag. Slowly, she unwrapped the dress. And then stepped aside.

My mouth dropped.

The dress was a champagne color and covered in irides-cent sequins. It was strapless and hugged the torso. Like the green dress, it was floor-length and had a slit up to the thigh. "What do you think?" Hope looked at me expectantly.

"Rachel." Gina breathed out my name.

"I know." We were both thinking the same thing. The dress was stunning.

"It's from Paris, I'm sure it's going to cost a lot."

"Well, like I said, there were only a limited number made. And in Charming, no one has seen it yet," Hope assured me.

She chewed on her bottom lip. She didn't offer to tell me the price. Bad sign.

"Okay," I said. "Then maybe I should look at the green dress."

Gina glared at me. "No, you are going to try on both dresses. And you're not going to look at the price tags because I'm sure it's not even on that dress. And then you are going to decide which one you really like. Not the one you think you can afford, or the dress you think you deserve. You are going to get the dress you really, really want."

I walked into the dressing room, and Hope followed behind me with the gowns in her hand. She hooked the green one on one hook and then hung the champagne-colored dream on the other. She closed the door behind her, leaving me alone.

I quickly shimmied out of my clothes down to my under-wear. I touched the green, silky dress first and took it off the rack. I slid it on and then zipped it up in the back. I turned and looked at my reflection in the mirror.

It hugged me perfectly.

The color was beautiful, and it fit like a dream.

It was a gorgeous dress. I knew it would look great for the charity event. I pulled the price tag out of the side and braced myself. Four hundred and fifty dollars. Wasn't that bad, considering it was for a formal event and imported from Paris. But I had always had a frugal side, and I didn't know if I could justify spending that much money.

I stepped out of the dressing room.

"Oh my gosh, that looks beautiful on you." And then Gina glared. "I would kill to have your tiny waist and little butt."

I rolled my eyes at my friend. "Gina, you are way slimmer than I am."

"That may be, but you still have curves. When I started running so much, I lost my butt. I kind of miss having it.

"So, go try on the other dress." She waved me back into the room.

"Fine, but do not get your hopes up. I'm sure that dress costs at least a thousand dollars."

I went back into the dressing room and quickly slid out of the green dress before I hung it up and then turned my attention to the champagne-colored gown.

I unzipped the side and stepped into the dress. Although it had sparkles and sequins, the inside was silky smooth. I zipped up the sides before turning to look at myself.

I reminded myself that the green dress was just as good as the one I had on. Probably didn't cost as much either. The color looked great on me. It didn't need to be altered. The green dress would do.

But as I turned, I reminded myself of how I always justified my choices in life. After I had found out about Miles' affair, I'd tried to make it work. I had tried to make do. In the end, I realized that wasn't me. I couldn't just make do, especially with a narcissistic asshole that really didn't regret hurting me or destroying his family.

I didn't have a whole lot of high expectations for this charity event, other than just a night out where I could dress up and maybe meet somebody I could have an adult conversation with. Perhaps it would turn into a date.

I closed my eyes and turned around to face the mirror.

I took a deep breath and opened my eyes.

I couldn't believe it. What I saw in the mirror was a totally different person.

Like the green dress, it had the slit, the color was perfect, and it fit me perfectly.

But unlike the green dress, it seemed to change my appearance. It made me feel like a queen. It made me look like a warrior.

I glanced down at the hem of the dress. It did not need any alterations or hemming. It was almost as if it was meant to be mine.

I opened the door and stepped out. Hope gasped, and Gina covered her mouth with her hand when she saw me.

"So, what do you guys think?"

"It's absolutely beautiful. It's almost like it was made especially for you." Hope clapped her hands excitedly.

I looked over at Gina. "Gina, you haven't said anything."

"That's because you took my breath away." She nodded her head slowly and looked at me. "Like literally took my breath away. You've got to get this dress, Rachel."

"Stand on the platform, Rachel," Gina urged.

I walked to the middle of the room and stepped onto the platform. I turned and looked at the floor-to-ceiling mirror.

"I have just the shoes for that gown." Hope ran out of the room. She reappeared seconds later with what looked like pumps made for a princess. They matched the dress and sparkled under the lights.

She bent and helped me slip my feet into the heels.

I stood straight and stared at my reflection in the mirror.

"You look stunning." Gina's eyes were big.

"You look perfect." Hope placed her hands under her chin and stared.

"I'm scared to even ask." My voice came out in a whisper. I was afraid of the disappointment I'd feel at not being able to afford the dress. I was scared of, once again, wanting something only to have it slip from my fingers.

"You realize this is more than a dress," Gina whispered. "It's a new turning point in your life. It will mark the point in time when you moved on from Miles."

"I know. But exactly how much is that going to cost me?" I turned and looked at Hope.

"The dress is three thousand dollars." Hope gave me a sheepish look.

I felt the blood drain from my face. "Holy shit. That's a lot of money."

"This is more than money, Rachel." Gina glared. "This is taking back your life and independence."

"Yeah, well, I didn't think it would cost me three thousand dollars." I glanced back at my reflection.

"I don't think I can sell that dress to anyone else." Hope's voice was soft with disappointment and hurt. "No one else could pull it off."

"She's right. Listen to Hope." Gina wrapped her arm around Hope's shoulders in solidarity.

Hope brightened. She had another ally on her side.

"I don't know… It's a lot of money."

Gina turned and looked at Hope. "Are you sure no one else in Charming has seen this dress?"

"No, no one…except…"

"Except who?" Gina grabbed her by the shoulder and gave her a shake. "Who, girl? Tell me."

"Easy, Gina." I took a step back. Gina had a feral look in her eyes. One I had never seen on her before.

Gina ignored me and glared at Hope. "Do you know her name?"

Hope looked from me back to Gina and spoke in a low voice. "I think everyone knows her name."

A chill ran down my spine. I knew who she was talking about.

"Hope, did Nikki Stollings look at this dress?"

Hope gave me a pained look. "She came in yesterday, very agitated. She said she wanted something new. Something that no one in Charming had worn or even seen. Said it was for a dating event."

"Are you fucking kidding me?" I addressed Gina.

Gina released Hope and glared back at me. "Don't start, Rachel."

"Is Nikki going to be part of this charity dating event?" I curled my hands into fists while my stomach turned. My vampire body didn't know whether to be angry or sick.

Gina took a deep breath. "It wasn't my idea. She got in before I knew about it. I want you to know that I told the committee how pissed I was about letting her in. They said they had more men entered than women, and she was attractive. So, they let her in."

"Let me get this straight. Nikki got in just because they needed more females?" I glared.

"So I've been told." Gina shook her head. "I swear, Rachel, if I had known they were going to let that bitch in, I never would have suggested that you enter. Or I would have at least tried to stop her from getting in."

I looked at my friend. My trust had been easily broken before. I was gun shy when it came to trust.

"Rachel, I know that look in your eyes. But let me tell you this much. I am your friend. I want you to do this charity event because there are a lot of great guys out there that could be great for you. Miles is not the only fish in the sea. He was a minnow. And you need a whale."

I snorted. "You're crazy. Do you know that?"

"My husband tells me that from time to time." Gina shrugged with an easy smile. "So, please tell me you will do this. You will stay in the dating event, and you will buy this dress."

I turned from my friend and looked at my reflection. Even with no makeup on and my hair hanging around my shoulders, I looked stunning. As if I could take on the world.

I turned back to Hope.

She looked as if she were holding her breath. She clasped her hands together under her chin again, and I thought for a second her eyes might be getting watery.

"Hope, I'll take the dress."

CHAPTER 22

*A*s soon as I paid for the dress and shoes with my credit card, Gina rushed me out of the store and into my car. I was pretty sure she was trying to get me out of there before I realized what an impulsive decision I had just made.

We had just pulled into the garage and gotten out of my Volvo when Miles pulled in behind me.

Gina stood beside me and folded her arms over her chest while he slid out of his Tesla.

"Miles, what are you doing here? It's not your weekend with the girls."

"I came over because I need something out of the attic." He slid a glance over at Gina. "Hello, Gina. How are you?"

"I was fine until about five seconds ago." She glared.

Miles blinked and took a step back. "Well, if you don't mind, I'll have a look around the attic."

"Let me back my car out first. I don't want the ladder to land on it."

The only way to get into the attic was by a ladder that

folded into the ceiling. When we first built the house, we had considered making the attic into an enormous playroom for the girls. But Miles thought it was foolish and a waste of space, considering we already had over seven-thousand feet of living area. So, we kept our Christmas decorations and things we couldn't bear to throw away in the attic.

"What are you getting out of the attic?" Gina cocked her head and studied him. I would have to tell her that she would have made a great attorney. She could intimidate a man in three-point-five seconds.

"If you must know, I need to get my old golf clubs down."

"I thought you sold those when I bought you the new ones." I had given him them as a birthday gift.

"I thought about it but figured I should just hold onto them in case the girls ever wanted to learn how to golf."

"Or you had another woman in mind to take golfing." Gina took a step towards Miles. "You've got a golf date. With a woman."

Miles' face turned bright red, and he looked at the ground. "Well, I..."

My stomach twisted. I was always amazed at myself for still having feelings for a man who had ripped out my heart. I guess once your heart was gone, it took time to heal the empty space.

"Miles, what you do now and who you do it with is none of my business." I shrugged.

"That's right." Gina nodded with a smirk. "In fact, we just got back from shopping for Rachel's dress for the charity event. You know the one, right?"

"Well, yes, I do." Miles cleared his throat.

"It's okay, Miles. I know you are going, too. Although I'm surprised. I thought you were dating someone." It was my turn to cross my arms over my chest.

"Yes, well, it didn't turn out so well." He shrugged.

"Are you talking about Nikki?" Gina glared.

"What? No. That's been over." He snorted.

"I think you should tell her that." Gina narrowed her eyes.

"Look, I don't have time for all this. I'm just here to grab my clubs and go." Miles walked around Gina and me, giving us both a wide berth. "Rachel, can you back your car out?"

I slid into my car and backed my Volvo out. Miles pulled the ladder down and made his way up.

"I can't believe you married someone like that." Gina shook her head.

"He wasn't always like this. At first, he was attentive and kind. I wonder if becoming a doctor and getting all that praise went to his head."

"I don't know, but let's get this dress inside before he sees it." Gina opened the car door and pulled out the gown. Hope had been so thrilled to sell the dress to me that she'd given me a huge discount on the shoes.

We headed inside and went straight to the bedroom closet. I hung up my purchase and put the shoes on the top shelf.

We walked back into the kitchen.

"Did you get something?" Arianna leaned on the island.

"I did. And I love it."

"Good." She smiled. "Is that Dad outside?"

"Yes, he is getting something out of the attic. He's taking his old golf clubs." I shut the closet door, and we walked into the living room.

"But he told me he was giving them to me." Arianna stopped and looked at me.

"Well, maybe he's just going to borrow them and bring them back." I gave her a tight smile.

"Or maybe he's just an asshole," Gina muttered.

Arianna went out the kitchen door to the garage.

"Shit. Should I go outside, or stay here? I'm still pretty new at this divorced co-parenting thing." I looked at Gina.

She shrugged. "I don't know, but if I go out there, it's going to be a screaming match. And me possibly beating his ass. It might scar Arianna, so I'm going to stay right here." Gina leaned against the counter.

I heard raised voices, so I decided I needed to go outside and see what was going on.

"You lied to me!" Arianna screamed. Tears streamed down her face.

"Honey, I don't remember promising you my old clubs. I think you are confused."

"The only thing that is confused is your integrity." Arianna turned and fled into the house.

I looked at Miles. "Did you promise the clubs to Arianna?"

"When she was five. And we were out in the yard playing around with the golf ball. I probably told her that then, but she hasn't shown any interest in golfing in years." He laughed. "She'll get over it."

My mouth dropped. "So you did promise her?"

"It wasn't really a promise. She was just a child." He shook his head and walked back to his vehicle and opened the trunk. He slid the clubs inside.

"She's still a child, Miles. She may be a teenager, but she remembers what you promise her."

He turned and glared at me. "Don't start. I had a long day of meetings."

"Tough shit." I shoved him in the middle of his chest. "You may be a doctor, but you are a father first and foremost. You need to remember that. I think you have your priorities mixed up."

"You're one to talk." He snorted and opened his car door.

"What does that mean?" I grabbed him by the arm.

"It means you are leaving your children to fend for themselves to go do God knows what." He snorted. "Don't you preach to me when you are guilty of it yourself."

He slid into his car and pulled out of my driveway. I turned around.

"That asshole didn't even put the ladder back up," I muttered.

I walked over and shoved the ladder back up into the ceiling. It was easy enough now that I was a vampire, but when I was human, it had been heavy.

I pulled my Volvo back into the garage. I went inside and found Gina consoling Arianna.

"Honey, I'm so sorry." I wrapped my arms around my child. She was almost as tall as I was now, but she'd always be my baby.

"He isn't the same." She pulled back and looked at me. "He's not the same father he used to be. I think someone sucked out his soul."

"That's exactly what happened. The medical term is midlife crisis." Gina patted her on the back.

"*Not helping*," I mouthed to her.

Gina shrugged.

I brushed Arianna's hair from her face. "Honey, do you really want some golf clubs? If you do, I can get you some."

She shook her head. "That's not the point. He promised them to me. And he lied. He took them back. How can a father take back a promise to a daughter? I don't understand him at all." Arianna wiped her tears and stormed off to her room.

I sighed.

"I need to go so you can defuse that." Gina patted me on the arm.

"Thanks, Gina. And thanks for everything you did today.

If you hadn't gone, I'm not sure I would have gotten that dress."

"That's what real friends are for." She headed out the door.

CHAPTER 23

The day of the Aces and Eights charity event had arrived. I had my hair done in beach waves, and my makeup professionally applied. I took another look at my reflection and smiled.

"Mom, you look amazing," Arianna said from the doorway of my bedroom. "Like, seriously. You look like a model."

"Thanks, sweetie. You sure you don't think it's too much?"

"Absolutely not. You are going to be the only woman at the event that will have all the men's attention."

"Lord, I hope." I snorted.

Her smile faded. "I bet Dad is going to be eating his heart out."

I was still upset about Miles taking her golf clubs. But I didn't want to fan that fire. As much as I wanted to.

"What time do you leave?" She changed the subject.

"Well, the shuttle will be here at five. It's an hour drive to Memphis, and we should be boarding the riverboat shortly after." I stifled a yawn.

"You don't seem very excited." She cocked her head.

"Sorry. I always have a late afternoon slump. I'll pick back up in a little while." The truth was the sunlight was draining me. Once the sun went down, I would get some energy back. It was my secret that was getting harder and harder to hide from my girls.

"So, is this going to be an all-night thing?" Gabby elbowed Arianna out of her way.

"Well, honey, I don't really know. It shouldn't go past midnight, but I'll have to wait for the shuttle to bring me back, so that's going to be another hour or so."

"Why are you doing this?" Gabby frowned.

My stomach dropped. Did she not approve? Did she think I was prioritizing them lower than myself? Did they think I was selfish like their father?

In that moment, the reality of how much I had spent on the dress sank in.

"Well, Gabby, I am doing this for a lot of reasons. I was hoping to find someone to talk to."

"You don't need to do this." Gabby scowled. "You have Khalan to talk to."

A laugh escaped my lips. Her scowl deepened.

"Khalan is my friend, and a lot of the time, I feel like I'm too much of a bother for him. So, maybe I can find someone tonight who likes my company."

"Oh, he likes your company just fine." Arianna gave a slight grin. "He seems super protective of you. Or maybe it's just stalker tendencies."

"Plus, he dresses cool, like a wizard." Gabby gave me a hard look. "I think Khalan is going to be jealous if you go."

I walked over and pulled both of my girls into a hug. "Thanks for that, Gabby and Arianna."

"For what?" Arianna pulled back enough to look at me.

"For thinking that maybe someone could love me again. Or at least get jealous over me again." A part of me wished I could tell them that it wasn't love that Khalan had for me. It was the obligation of a Maker.

Gabby took a step back and looked at me, obviously still not happy about my decision to go to the event.

"You know what else? No matter what happens or who I meet, you girls are always first in my life. You both know that, right?"

" Yes," they said in long-suffering unison.

The doorbell rang.

I stiffened. "Maybe I shouldn't go."

"You are going." Arianna shoved me out of the bedroom towards the living room. My heels clacked against the hard-wood floor.

The doorbell rang again. I turned and looked at my girls. "Gabby?" I needed to know that she was okay with me going.

"You should go." Gabby nodded. "You look beautiful, and you don't want to waste your hair and makeup on just staying home." She shrugged. "Besides, that's all you ever do is stay in whenever you aren't running us around." She grabbed my black clutch off the coffee table and handed it to me along with my cell phone.

"I'm nervous," I admitted and stuck my phone into my bag.

"You'll be fine," Arianna encouraged. "Besides, I'm kind of liking watching the house while you're gone."

"And I hate it." Gabby shot daggers at her sister.

"Don't fight. And you have my number if you need anything." I glanced around with the feeling that I was forgetting something.

"We will be fine. Gabby just needs to learn that I'm in charge when you're gone." She smirked.

"Yeah, right," Gabby shot back.

The doorbell rang again.

Arianna shook her head and walked over and opened the door.

I almost forgot to breathe.

Standing on the other side of the door was Jack, the werewolf, wearing a suit and a chauffeur hat. A grin stretched across his face when he saw me.

"What are you doing here?" I stared. My heart rate sped up a little at the sight of him. He looked pretty hot in a suit.

"I'm your chauffeur for the night." He grinned wickedly.

"Do you know the driver?" Arianna looked between us.

"A little," I admitted. "Don't wait up for me, and Gabby, listen to your sister." I gave them both a quick kiss on the forehead and walked out the front door before they could ask me any more questions.

I hurried down towards the driveway.

"That was disappointing. I didn't get an introduction to your girls. Who, by the way, are just as beautiful as their mother." Jack's deep voice slid across my body.

I shook my head and then stopped at the long vehicle parked in my driveway. I spun around and looked at him. "What's this?"

He gave me an odd look. "It's a limousine."

"No, shit. I know it's a limousine. I thought they were sending a shuttle."

"Well, apparently, for this event, they wanted to do it in style. So, no bus shuttle for you." He walked over to the door and opened it.

"Am I your only pick-up?"

"No. I picked up another hot chick. She'll be riding with you to the charity event."

"Perfect." I lifted the hem of my dress to get in.

He grabbed my arm and pulled me a little closer.

My heart squeezed in my chest. Jack seemed to have that effect on me, especially when he was in my personal space.

He leaned closer. His eyes bore into mine. "You look beautiful tonight."

"Thank you."

"You know, I could drop the other chick off at the event and me and you could go have dinner."

I had to admit that what Jack was saying sounded good to me. But I also knew there was something about him that I couldn't trust. Or maybe it was just the fact that I had been betrayed before and wasn't ready to get my heart broken. Jack may affect my body, but I wouldn't let him touch my brain.

He released my arm, and I ducked and slid into the back of the limousine.

"What the hell are you doing here?" I glared at Nikki, who was sitting across from me. The door slammed behind me, locking me in with my worst enemy.

Nikki jerked her head up and looked at me with wide eyes.

"I asked you what you're doing here?"

"Well, I could ask you the same thing," she stammered.

"I was invited to this event." I narrowed my eyes at her. "You do realize that this is a dating event, right? I mean, you're technically still married to Brad."

She lifted her chin defiantly and clasped her hands in her lap. She was wearing a sleeveless red dress that came just below her knees.

I should have known an adulteress would wear red. Which made me glad I had chosen the dress I had on.

"Technically, I'm still married. But as everybody knows, Brad left a suicide note. So, I thought I would go to the event to see if I could find someone to talk to."

"Bullshit. I don't believe you're going just to find somebody to talk to. I think you're going to find somebody to take care of you."

She pressed her lips into a thin, white line and held my gaze. "You do realize I work, Rachel. I've always worked."

"Yeah, and I know that Brad worked two jobs to keep you in the lifestyle you grew accustomed to. And when that didn't suit you, you went after my husband." I cocked my head and studied her. "You're not going to find somebody new, you are attending to see who Miles chooses."

"I cared a lot for Miles. I still do."

The car lurched into motion, backing down the driveway. Half of me wanted to escape, to jump out of the car, duck and roll, and scramble back into the house. The other half knew that I was in an enclosed space with Nikki, and I could beat her ass, and nobody would know what had happened. In fact, I could probably kill her and hide her body.

"You've got a lot of fucking nerve telling me how you loved *my* husband, while I was married to him. You know, I don't think I've ever met a sociopath. But I think I'm looking at one right now. And I'm going to tell you something, you and Miles are not getting back together. For the simple fact that I don't want you anywhere near my daughters. I think you are a dangerous person, and I will do whatever I need to in order to protect them."

She narrowed her eyes slightly and, for the first time, I could see anger hiding behind the perfect mask she always presented to the world.

She opened her mouth to say something, but I looked deep into her eyes. I leaned forward and held her gaze.

"Nikki, I'm going to ask you some questions, and I want you to be honest with me."

Her eyes glazed over, and the tension around her mouth relaxed. I could tell she was falling under my glamour.

"Nikki, tell me why you had an affair with Miles."

She looked at me without blinking. "He was showing me attention when Brad didn't. Brad worked long hours and was too tired to do anything fun. And I was tired of always struggling for money."

"Nikki, did you love Miles?"

"I loved it when Miles brought me flowers. I loved it when Miles brought me gifts. I loved it when Miles took on trips. To places that Brad could never afford."

It was like a slap in the face. I knew he had taken that bitch to the medical conference out of state. But I only found that out after I glamoured the surgical techs at the party at the country club.

"Nikki, where did Miles take you?"

"Two trips to Vegas, one trip to the Florida Keys. And a trip to the Bahamas."

"Motherfucker." I leaned back in my seat and tried to take in the information she had just given me. While I had been at home with the kids, he'd been out doing whatever he wanted and going wherever he wanted. For the first time since getting a divorce, I was glad I had blown the money on the dress I was wearing. I regretted not treating myself to more while we were married. I had grown up in the foster system, and I always wanted to provide financial security for my girls. I didn't want them to have to worry about money. I didn't want them to be afraid of the world, like I had been.

I leaned forward, composed myself, and held her gaze again.

"Nikki, you won't remember answering the questions I asked you. You won't remember the questions I asked you about Miles."

"I understand." She nodded slowly. I rested my hands in my lap and glanced away, breaking the glamour I had on her.

CHAPTER 24

*W*e rode for several minutes in silence, avoiding each other's gazes.

The limo slowed down. I looked out the window. We pulled up to a sprawling home with large, white columns. I immediately recognized the house as being located in an older neighborhood in Charming. I remembered seeing it when I'd gone there for a Halloween party a few years back. I had dressed as a sexy nurse, and Miles had dressed as a priest.

It was ironic, thinking back on it now. We were both wearing masks that the other couldn't see.

The limo stopped, and I met Jack's gaze in the rearview mirror.

"We have to pick up a few more people before heading to the riverboat." He gave me a wink before he got out.

"Do you know the driver?" Nikki cocked her head.

"A little," I murmured.

"That's not what Veronica said."

I jerked my head in her direction. She crossed her arms and lifted her chin.

"I don't give a shit what Veronica said." I narrowed my eyes, daring her to say something else.

I was not in the mood for it today.

The limo door opened, and Jack peeked his head inside. "A gentleman is going to be riding with us, ladies. He's on his way out." Jack smiled at Nikki and then at me. His gaze lingered on me a little too long to be comfortable.

"How many other stops do we have to make?" I clasped my hands together in my lap and tried not to shift in my seat.

"One more." He winked. "Have I told you how beautiful you look tonight?"

"Yes. You did." I tried to look away, but my body would not obey. Apparently, it really liked looking at the hot werewolf.

"It needs to be said again and again." His smile spoke of wicked promises.

My face turned red, and my stomach warmed. It had definitely been too long since I'd been with a man. Maybe I didn't need to be dating. Perhaps I just needed a good roll in the sack.

Jack seemed to be reading my thoughts.

I looked away.

Jack stepped back from the door, and a gray head poked inside the limo.

"Well, hello, ladies." A gentleman in his late sixties grinned from ear to ear. He was wearing a seersucker suit and a flaming red bowtie. He slid into the limo, sitting next to Nikki. "My name is Earl. Earl Hackett." He held out his hand to me, and I took it.

"I'm Rachel Jones." I smiled politely. I pulled my hand out of his sweaty grip.

"Pleasure is all mine." His gaze slid across my body.

I sat back as far as I could on the seat and crossed my

arms over my chest. His gaze lingered on the long slit up my thigh.

"Nikki Stollings." Nikki smiled and held out her hand.

Earl dragged his gaze from me to her. Suddenly, his face lit up. "Nikki. I like it. It's a pretty name." He edged closer to her and leered.

Nikki patted his arm and smiled. "Very nice suit. It's a classic."

"Well, thank you, my dear. I've had this suit since I met my wife. She was never much of a fashionista, and she didn't like it. But after she died a few months ago, I decided to resurrect it." He grinned.

I cringed.

Nikki cocked her head slightly and smiled.

Jack poked his head into the car. His laser gaze tracked straight to me.

"How many other people are we picking up?" I muttered.

"Two more." He nodded in Earl's direction. "If he gives you any problems, I'll pull over and beat his ass."

Earl chuckled. "I bet I can take you, whippersnapper."

"Try it, old man." Jack glared.

"It's fine." I tried shoving Jack's head out of the door. "Just go pick up the rest of the group so we can get to the boat."

He grabbed my hand and pressed his lips to my palm. His tongue darted out and licked ever so slightly. I gasped and squeezed my thighs together.

I still had enough presence of mind to force my body to obey me. I snatched my hand away and glared.

He grinned, gave me another wink, and shut the door.

"That's a very protective boyfriend you got there." Earl chortled. "I was never much for associating with the help."

Nikki snorted.

I bristled. "At least, he's single. It could be worse. I could be messing around with a married man."

I looked straight at Nikki.

She glared and then looked away.

Earl looked from me to her. "There's a whole lot of tension in this car. I bet you two are best friends and had a falling out."

"We are most definitely not friends." I looked out the window as Jack pulled back onto the street.

"I think you are. I used to be a sports agent before I retired and moved to Charming."

Great. Just what I needed.

"You are mistaken," Nikki emphasized.

"I think you are both lying." Earl crossed his arms over his seersucker-clad chest and studied us both. "You may not be friends now, but at one time, you were."

"Maybe. But that was a long time ago," Nikki said softly.

It was the first time I'd heard any kind of emotion in her voice.

I jerked my head in her direction.

"See, I told you I was right. Tell me what happened, and I can help you work through it."

"There's nothing to work through. Some things are just too broken to fix." I looked at him, daring him to say another word.

Thankfully, I was spared another lecture from Earl because Jack eased the limo to a stop.

We stopped in front of Emerald's Luxury Apartments. They were the nicest rentals in Charming and housed executives visiting for business.

Who in the world were we picking up?

I watched Jack as he ambled up to the front door and knocked. The door opened, but I couldn't see who was on the other side. Jack's large frame was in my way.

JACK TURNED and walked back to the limo. His gaze locked on mine.

Could he see me through the tinted windows?

I turned away as the heat rose in my cheeks.

The door opened. I averted my gaze.

"Hello."

The hair on the back of my neck stood at attention.

I knew that voice.

The door slammed.

"Dr. Kramer. I wasn't expecting to see you tonight." I forced a polite smile.

"Rachel." He didn't look surprised to see me.

"You two know each other?" Earl looked from me to Dr. Kramer.

"Yes. We do." Dr. Kramer looked at Earl and held out his hand. "I'm Dr. Milton Kramer. Nice to meet you."

"I'm Earl Hackett." He gave him a handshake. "What kind of doctor are you?"

"A psychiatrist." Dr. Kramer trained his gaze on me.

"So, are you a patient of his?" Earl grinned broadly.

"I most certainly am not." I glared.

Earl chucked. "I didn't mean any offense. I mean, I think going to a headshrinker is good."

Dr. Kramer wrinkled his nose at the derogatory name. "That's a very offensive term. And I don't appreciate it."

Earl lost his grin and rolled his eyes. "That's what's wrong with the world today. Everyone is so damn offended all the time. Isn't that right?" He elbowed Nikki.

Nikki blinked several times and stuttered.

"It's not about being offended. It's about manners and common decency. Something this world doesn't have enough of."

"I think you need a drink." Earl opened the mini bar in the limo. He poured some scotch into a highball glass.

Jack maneuvered the limo back onto the street.

"I don't drink." He lifted his chin in the air, refusing the peace offering that Earl tried to hand to him.

"More for me." He tossed back the liquor and refilled his glass. "Ladies, can I offer you two a cocktail?"

"I don't drink scotch. But thank you."

"You don't drink, Rachel? At all? Or does your taste run to something more...rare." Dr. Kramer's eyes glinted with a shared secret.

"Ah. I know what she likes." Earl winked.

I froze. My blood ran cold, and my heart almost stopped in my chest.

"Yeah. You like that Riesling. That sweet wine." Earl folded his hands across his chest and looked pretty pleased with himself.

"Actually, she hates sweet wine. She likes red." Nikki shook her head.

All eyes were on me.

"Well? Is that right?"

"Yes. I love red wine. But lately..."

"Lately, your tastes have changed. Isn't that right, Rachel?" Dr. Kramer's eyes were burning me to my core.

I cleared my throat. "Actually, I was going to say that I haven't been drinking a whole lot of wine lately at all."

"Tastes have changed, have they?" Dr. Kramer looked at me.

"See, I knew it." Earl clapped his hands together.

"Knew what?" How much longer was this car ride from Hell going to last?

"That you and Nikki are best friends. And whatever has caused you to fall out, should be put aside and forgiven. I've lived a long time on this Earth, and I know a good friend is hard to find."

"This is a different situation." I fidgeted in my seat.

Nikki stayed silent and kept her gaze averted out the window.

Dr. Kramer seemed to finally notice that Nikki was in the car. "Nikki Stollings, is it?"

"Yes. Nice to meet you," she said politely. The smile she wore on her face didn't reach her eyes. She was as uncomfortable as I was.

"Aren't you the one whose husband committed suicide not that long ago?" Dr. Kramer cocked his head.

"Wow. You don't let the grass grow under your feet, do you, honey?" Earl slapped his knee. "That's the way it should be. Life's too short. Got to leave the living to those with a pulse."

"It's not like that." She lifted her chin in the air. "I don't know that he's really dead. The body was never found. All he left was a note."

"Think he ran off with another woman?" Earl prodded.

I snorted. Nikki jerked her gaze back to me.

"So, you're saying your husband left a suicide note, and yet there's no evidence that he's actually dead?" Earl cocked his head.

"Right." Nikki nodded slowly.

I was glad the focus was off me and now on her. I pulled my cell phone out of my clutch and checked the time.

"Do you have any enemies, Mrs. Stollings?" Dr. Kramer's tone set my teeth on edge.

She cut her eyes at me. "Normally, no."

"Why, you don't consider Rachel your enemy, do you?" Earl took another drink of his scotch.

Dr. Kramer studied the tension between us. He narrowed his eyes on me.

"Wait. Aren't you the one who slept with Rachel's husband?"

Earl choked on his scotch. "Wait. What?"

Nikki's face went white.

"Yes. And I don't want to talk about it." I crossed my arms. This was supposed to be a night of new beginnings, and all we were talking about was the past.

I was tired of it.

"Did you stay with the bastard?" Earl leaned forward in his seat.

"We're divorced." I gave him a hard stare.

"Wait, is his name Miles Jones?" Earl pulled out his cell phone and punched in some numbers.

"Yes."

"And he's going to be at the charity event, as well." Earl's eyes sparkled like fireworks.

The urge to throw the man and his ugly ass seersucker suit out the moving limo was overwhelming.

"So I've heard." I gritted my teeth.

Earl looked at Nikki. "Are you there to keep an eye on him to make sure he doesn't put his stinger in another flower?"

Nikki's face went red, and her eyes nearly bulged out of her head.

"Ha!" Earl pointed his liver-spotted finger at her. "That's exactly what you're doing. I knew it." He laughed and slapped his leg.

I bristled. I pushed the button and rolled down the barrier between Jack and us.

"How much longer?" I snapped.

His gaze met mine in the rearview mirror. "What's wrong? You guys not having stimulating conversation?"

"No." Everyone except Earl answered in unison.

"You will be glad to know we are almost there." He winked.

I pushed the button. Jack kept his gaze on me until the barrier went back up.

"I think our driver has a thing for you, Rachel." Earl waggled his eyebrows.

"Humph." Dr. Kramer crossed his arms and looked out the window.

"Is that so?" Nikki smirked. I supposed she was glad she wasn't the topic of conversation anymore.

"I assure you, I don't know what you mean." I crossed my arms and glared at the carful of enemies surrounding me.

I felt the limo slow to a stop, and I allowed myself to breathe.

We had finally arrived.

CHAPTER 25

I reached for the door handle, but Jack was faster. He must have seen my distress at being surrounded by a car full of people that I didn't want to be around. He opened the door, and I scrambled out ungracefully.

I took two steps towards the riverboat and stopped. I had seen the boat many times when in Memphis, but I had never been inside of it.

It was larger than I imagined it would be. The red and white and blue colors splashed across the sides reminded me of the Fourth of July.

I had read in the paper that they'd recently remodeled the interior of the boat. I was hoping it would live up to my expectations.

"Are you excited for tonight?" Jack grinned down at me.

He was standing so close, his arm rubbed my shoulder.

I took my gaze off him and looked back at the boat. "You know, I've lived close to Memphis practically all my life, and I've never actually been on the riverboat."

"I've been just about everywhere in the world. I've seen bigger vessels." Jack grinned at me.

"Really? I thought wolves lived in Packs and pretty much stayed in one place."

"Most wolves do." The tone of his voice gave me shivers.

"I'm not like most wolves," he added.

"So Khalan has said."

"Khalan has been talking about me, has he?" Jack's tone hardened.

"I didn't say that." Khalan was my Maker, and my loyalty was to him. Despite my attraction to Jack.

I scanned the balcony of the riverboat and spotted Gina. Her gaze landed on me, and she gave me a wave.

I waved back, relieved to finally see somebody I recognized. Somebody I actually liked.

A gentleman dressed in a black tux walked down the gangplank in my direction.

"You must be Rachel Jones. We are so pleased to have you joining us tonight. My name is Ralph Perkins. I am one of the co-chairs for the committee." He held out his hand.

I shook it and smiled politely. "Thank you for having me. You know, this is my first time doing something like this."

"The dating, or something for charity?"

"Both, actually." We both laughed.

"If you would just follow me up the gangplank, we will actually leave the dock in about fifteen minutes."

"Are we the last ones to arrive?"

I hated being late.

"We are waiting on one more guest to arrive. He is on his way. Then we are leaving. But if you just go inside, Gina will show you around, and we can get started."

I glanced around but didn't see Jack. I didn't wait around for Nikki to catch up with me, I just headed for the gangplank.

My heels clacked against the wood of the boat. I glanced down at the water, noting its muddy color.

"Welcome to the Aces and Eights Charity Dating Event." A young waiter dressed in a tux held out a silver tray of champagne flutes.

"Thank you" I took a glass and stepped to the side. I glanced behind me and saw Nikki following.

I needed to get away. I couldn't stand being confined with her again. It was weird how you could think you knew someone all your life, only to find that they could betray you in such a way.

I walked inside the interior of the riverboat. Everything on the inside had most definitely been replaced. The carpet was a deep red, the walls had been recovered with a cream-colored wallpaper, and the original crown molding had been refurbished.

The inside had been decorated like a casino that dated back to the old Wild West times.

Several card tables were set up for poker along with dealers, roulette tables, and even some slot machines where you actually had to pull the handle to make them work.

Men and women were already coupled up, talking over their glasses of champagne. There were a few stragglers around the room, those either too shy to make conversation or perhaps waiting to see who else was boarding before they attempted to meet anyone.

"Rachel, what do you think of the event?" Dr. Kramer stepped up to me with a glass of bourbon.

I cringed and took a step away from him. I didn't want anybody thinking I was with him, and I certainly didn't want to be around him if he knew what I was.

"I think it's a lovely event. I hope that you find someone to talk to. Who knows, maybe you will find the love of your life tonight?" I took a step away. His fat hand clamped down on my elbow.

I spun around and glared at him. He leaned in close. "You're a fool if you think I'm here for anything other than to observe and catch you."

"Catch me doing what? Having a cocktail?" I glared.

"Don't you realize that tonight is a full moon? And when that happens, you're going to be overrun with bloodlust. I'm here to make sure everybody knows exactly what you are."

"You're crazy." I jerked out of his grasp and hurried into the next room. Thankfully, it was more crowded, and I quickly lost him.

There were tablecloth-covered tables here, and people were sitting in assigned seats. I walked around the room, looking for my name. I found my seat and sat. Luckily, there were other people already at the table. They had arranged the seating, alternating male and female. I was sure it was to facilitate conversation and to get us to meet different people. I sat between two men in their late forties. "Well, hello," the man to my right greeted me. "My name is John Wallace." He held out his hand.

I shook it and smiled back. "I'm Rachel Jones. Nice to meet you. It looks like we've got one more person boarding before we can get going."

"Ahh, so that's what we're waiting for. I've been here for about forty-five minutes. But I don't mind the wait. They've got excellent cocktails, and the conversation has been even better."

"I thought we would be early, but apparently not." I looked at the gentleman to my left.

"Hi, I'm Rachel Jones."

He grinned manically and held out his hand. "My name is Mark Rutledge."

The other people at our table had paired up and were in deep conversation. I didn't want to interrupt them just to introduce myself. I was content to sit back and watch the room. And keep an eye on Dr. Kramer.

CHAPTER 26

The waiter began placing salads in front of everyone seated at our table. I picked up my napkin and placed it in my lap before reaching for my water glass.

"Would you care for a cocktail or a glass of wine?"

I looked up at the waiter and nearly choked. It was Jack.

"You're a waiter, as well?" I cocked my head.

"It was the only way I could think of to get on the boat." He lowered his head next to mine. "The only way I could get close to you."

I cleared my throat, and the two men sitting next to me narrowed their eyes on Jack.

"I'll have a glass of Cabernet."

"Of course." Jack winked and headed over to the bar on the far side of the room.

"I'm surprised at how flirty the help is." John raised his eyebrows.

"I'm sure he's like that with everyone. Not just me." I gave him a strained smile.

I didn't want any more drama tonight. Just a night of relaxing conversation and, hopefully, maybe a future date.

"So, what do you do for a living, Rachel?" John took a bite of salad.

"I'm…a stay-at-home mom." I almost said, *"photographer for a private investigator,"* but that was something very few people knew about. It was better that way.

"I see." He seemed a little confused.

"I was a housewife until my divorce. Now, I'm a stay-at-home mom and take care of my two girls."

"I see," he said again and nodded.

"What do you do?" I asked.

Jack appeared and placed my wine in front of me. He lingered a little too long before leaving the table. From the corner of my eye, I noticed he didn't wait on anyone else. Instead, he hung around the bar.

John looked around. Finally, he flagged down a waiter and ordered a glass of wine.

He turned back to me. "I'm an accountant. I live in Memphis and have several firms around the Southeast."

"How nice." I nodded. "You must be very busy."

"I am. My mother keeps telling me I'm not getting any younger." He shook his head. "I'll be fifty in a few years, and I haven't found time to settle down and get married."

"If business is your passion, then you shouldn't have any regrets." God knew marriage had not worked out for me.

"What about you? Do you plan on getting married again?" He took another bite and studied me.

"Me?" I laughed. "No. I really don't think marriage is in my future."

"So, why are you here?" John leaned back in his chair.

The question caught me off guard. "Well, I thought this would be a great way to get back into dating. Nothing serious. Just someplace to find someone I can have some great conversation with and maybe a date." I took another drink of my wine.

"What about you? What are your expectations for this night?" I turned it back on him.

"I'm hoping to find a wife. Have some kids." He nodded his head. "Do you want any more kids?"

"No. I think I'm good in the kid department."

"I see." He turned his attention to the middle-aged woman who sat on the other side of him.

I bristled at being dismissed so quickly. It was pretty fucking rude of him to do that. It wasn't like he was the cat's meow. I mean, he wasn't that good-looking, and he was starting to lose his hair. I couldn't imagine that he would even be good around kids.

"Hi. My name is William, and I'm a dentist." The man next to me smiled.

He had broccoli stuck in his teeth. But at least they were white.

"How exciting." I tried not to yawn. It wasn't dark yet, and I was fading. I needed the sun to go down all the way to get my energy back.

"Is your practice in Memphis?" I asked politely and pushed my salad around my plate.

"It is. But I'm thinking of opening a second one in Charming. If I had a reason to move there." He waggled his bushy eyebrows at me.

I shifted in my seat and downed my wine.

"Looks like you need a refill." Jack appeared at my side with a bottle of wine. Without asking, he filled up my glass.

"Thank you." I took a deep drink.

"You know, if you're not really hungry, there are other events going on in the next room. Gambling in particular," Jack suggested.

"Really?" I smiled at William. "If you'll excuse me."

"But you've not had your entrée." His face fell.

"I'm not really hungry. Feel free to have it."

135

He gave me a wide smile. "Thanks."

I grabbed my clutch and hurried out of the room.

I stepped out onto the balcony of the riverboat. The sun had dipped below the horizon, and we were slowly pulling away from the dock.

"You look beautiful." Jack put his hand on my lower back.

"You already said that. Several times."

"It bears repeating." He leaned in close.

I rested my arm on the railing and turned. "How did you get changed so fast? First, a chauffeur's suit and now a waiter's? Did they hire you twice for both jobs?"

He grinned slowly. "No. they hired me as a driver. I paid for this uniform."

"Why would you do that?" I laughed. "Do you like serving people?"

"No, but I would love to serve you." He leaned in close.

His scent swept over me and made me almost whimper.

His finger trailed up my naked arm. "I know you like me. And you have to know that you stole my heart the minute I set eyes on you in the woods."

My heart hammered in my chest. White noise blared between my ears.

"Woods? What on earth were you doing in the woods, Rachel?" Dr. Kramer's voice raked over me like nails on a chalkboard.

"She was with me." Jack glared.

"Hmmm. Likely story." Dr. Kramer took a drink and pushed his glasses up to the bridge of his nose.

"I think I'll go inside. If you will excuse me." I walked past Dr. Kramer and heard Jack growl behind me. Apparently, he was not pleased about being interrupted. As much as I disliked Dr. Kramer, it was for the best that he'd walked up.

I liked Jack. I liked him a little too much. I wasn't here to get my heart broken. I was looking for someone I could have a stable relationship with. Nothing serious. Who knew, I might even find my best friend here tonight.

I walked into the gambling room and glanced around. People were busy talking and playing cards. I grabbed another glass of wine from a passing waiter and made my way across the room.

I noticed how the men turned and looked when I passed by. It bolstered my self-esteem. I felt someone's eyes on my back.

The hair on the back of my neck stood at attention.

I turned.

From across the room, and dressed in a fitted tux, stood Khalan.

My mouth dropped. He looked absolutely gorgeous. He had trimmed his beard and cut his hair to his shoulders. His deep blue eyes seared me from where I stood.

My heart raced in my chest.

Slowly, he made his way over, prowling towards me like a lion stalks his prey.

"Khalan."

"Rachel." The way he said my name almost made me go weak in the knees.

"What are you doing here?" I pressed my hand to my throat and looked around.

A few people were watching us. Probably watching *him* because he looked pretty damn hot.

"I'm here because…"

"Khalan." Jack elbowed his way between us. "What the fuck are you doing here?"

"Why is everyone asking me that?" Khalan growled. A passing waiter gave him a wide berth.

"You're not exactly the social type." Jack lifted his chin.

Khalan looked at Jack's uniform and shoved his empty champagne flute at him. "Make yourself useful and get me a drink."

"Sure, how about a nice glass of fuck off?" Jack smiled broadly.

"Excuse me, but is there a problem?" Ralph walked over to us.

"Yes. There is. My waiter isn't being helpful," Khalan deadpanned.

"My apologies, sir. What was it you wanted again?" Jack pasted on a smile.

"Bourbon would be great." Khalan glared.

Jack snatched the flute out of my Maker's hand and marched over to the bar.

"My apologies. He was a last-minute replacement." Ralph gave Khalan a pained look.

"I understand. It really is hard to find good help these days." Khalan kept his gaze on me.

Ralph left us alone.

"What are you doing with Jack? I told you to stay away from him." Khalan stepped into my personal space and glared down at me.

"I'm not with him," I hissed between my teeth. Khalan may be hot, but I was pissed.

"He picked me up in the limo, along with some others. I had no idea he was going to be working on the boat, as well." I glanced back at the bar. Jack lifted a glass and downed the substance. I figured he was drinking out of Khalan's glass.

"He's not here to work. He's here to get you into his bed." Khalan growled.

"What? That's ridiculous." I swallowed and pressed my hand to my neck.

"Is it? When I got on the boat, I smelled you on him. He probably stole some of your panties and rubbed your scent all over his body. Like a typical dog would do."

"What? No. I have never let him into my house."

"You said he picked you up." His eyes hardened.

"He did, but he met me at the door, and I certainly didn't invite him in." I lifted my chin. "I don't know why you're making such a big deal out of this."

"I don't know why you aren't smart enough to see what he wants from you."

"And what is that?"

"To get inside your panties," Khalan hissed.

"You're such a dick." My smile slipped, and I glanced around. We had attracted the attention of a few couples in the room, who had stopped gambling and were now looking our way.

"Now, everyone is staring at us." I lowered my voice and forced a smile.

"They are not staring at us. They are staring at *you*."

Jack returned with bourbon in a highball glass. "Here you are, sir. Hope it's to your liking." Jack gave Khalan a smartass salute.

My Maker ignored Jack and kept his gaze glued to me. He lifted the glass to his lips and took a sip. He let out a low growl. "It's fucking scotch. I hate scotch."

"Rachel!"

I turned as Gina made her way across the room to me. She gave me a kiss on the cheek. "I'm so glad you're here." She stepped back and looked at my dress. "You look absolutely amazing. Doesn't she?" She looked at Khalan.

"Breathtaking," Khalan said, low and deep.

If he hadn't been glaring at me, I would have almost believed he meant it. Instead, he looked like he wanted to wring my neck.

"I see you've already made a friend, Rachel." Gina was now focused on Khalan. Her eyes seemed to glaze over a little, and she flashed him a grin.

Gina was crushing on Khalan.

"I'm Khalan." He turned his attention to my friend and held out his hand. Immediately, I tensed.

She took it and giggled. "I'm Gina."

"And she's married," I reminded her.

"Oh, of course, I'm married." She laughed and gave me serious side-eye. "I don't remember seeing you on our list of eligible bachelors."

"It was last-minute. I hope that hasn't inconvenienced you."

"Absolutely not. We love surprises. Isn't that right, Rachel?"

I wrinkled my nose. Gina was acting like a high school girl crushing on the quarterback.

"Rachel?" She turned to me.

"I hate surprises. Always have. Now, if you will excuse me, I have some mingling to do." I shoved my clutch under my arm and winced when the sequins scraped across my bare flesh.

I strode across the room with my head held high. I thought I heard Khalan's low, disapproving growl, which lifted my spirits.

I walked out onto the deck and made my way to the

back of the boat. No one was out except for me. They were all enjoying themselves inside, gambling or stuffing their faces.

This was a mistake. I never should have come tonight.

"I thought I would find you out here." Dr. Kramer's voice broke the peace of the night.

"Ugh." I turned. I was all out of good manners. "What do you want? Don't you have women inside to meet and possibly marry?"

"I didn't come here for a date." He cringed.

"Then why the hell are you here?" I narrowed my eyes.

"I'm here to catch you turning into a vampire. It's a full moon tonight, and that's when you are at your most vulnerable. Once I have proof of what you are, I can convince the jury that my patient was under mind control at the time of the murder."

I stepped back. His words hit me like a slap across the face.

His lips slid into a grin. "I can tell by your reaction that I'm telling the truth." He clamped his hand across my wrist.

Pain bit into my skin. "Let go. You're hurting me." I tried to scream, but I felt the energy leaving my body like smoke.

"Not until I get what I came for. And don't try to fight it. The silver ring I'm wearing is what is piercing your skin. You will become weaker by the minute." He shoved me towards a door marked *Private*. He grabbed the keys out of his pants' pocket and shoved the key into the lock while keeping a tight grip on my wrist.

The door swung open, and he shoved me inside.

I felt to the floor in a heap. He turned the light on.

We were in a bedroom. The room was decorated in shades of red with a large canopy bed in the middle of the room. There were silver chains attached to the corners of the bed.

"Let's go." He pulled me up and shoved me onto the mattress.

All I wanted to do was sleep. I had never been so tired in my life.

He grabbed my arm and chained it to one post of the bed. The silver wasn't piercing my skin so it didn't hurt as much. But it did make my skin sting like a sunburn.

"Hey, what are you doing?" I tried to get away, but my body would not cooperate.

"I'm chaining you up." He secured my other arm with the silver chain and then proceeded to tether my ankles.

When he was done, he stood at the foot of the bed and looked at me. "There. That should hold you. You are too weak to scream, and the silver will continue to suck the energy out of you. Once that's down, and the full moon is up, your true nature will come out. Along with your fangs."

"You are crazy," I argued. "I don't have fangs."

"Stop lying. All vampires have fangs. I'm not an idiot, you know."

"You are an idiot if you think I'm a vampire."

"Oh, yeah? Then why is your energy draining with the silver? That's typical vampire stuff."

"I'm tired because I had one too many cocktails. And I'm a mom. Try parenting all on your own and see if you aren't exhausted."

He glanced at his watch and sighed. "I'll be back. I'm going to get in a round of poker before the unveiling happens." He clasped his hands together. "I can't imagine what everyone here tonight will think once they know your secret. I'll be the hero and clear Cal's good name."

"Cal doesn't have a good name. He's a murderer. And you are an asshole with too much time on your hands. No wonder you don't have a wife. No one could put up with your shit."

His face turned bright red.

Usually, I was considerate of people's feelings. But Dr. Kramer wasn't human. He was evil.

CHAPTER 28

*A*lone in the room, tears slid down my cheeks. I hardly ever cried. Hell, I didn't have time for crying. But now, alone in a room and tied down with silver, I was scared.

Would the moon affect me? It hadn't before. And how did I not know about silver being harmful to me?

Khalan was going to get an earful when I got my ass out of this situation.

I opened my mouth to scream, but all that came out was a barely audible hoarse whimper.

Could Khalan hear me? In the past when I'd needed him, I simply closed my eyes, and he could feel my pain and would come.

I squeezed my eyes shut and concentrated on him.

Khalan, Khalan, Khalan.

I opened my eyes, expecting to see him in front of me.

The room was empty.

No one was coming. I had to get myself out of this mess.

I tried to pull my arm away from the silver chain. I

focused all my strength on that one task. I moved my arm an inch. The silver held.

I stared up at the ceiling. Caught between exhaustion and terror, I felt as if I were going to have a heart attack at any moment.

Who would take care of my girls once I was gone? Miles was too busy repairing his image and chasing women to be a full-time, devoted dad. I had been raised in an orphanage after my parents died in a fire when I was little. So the girls didn't have grandparents. Miles' dad had died at an early age, and his mom hated my guts. She'd always felt like Miles had married beneath his station. So, she'd basically cut us out of her life. Last I heard, she was living in Italy with her rich boyfriend.

Tears stung the backs of my eyes, and pain cut across my heart like a sharp knife.

I wasn't ready to leave my girls. I couldn't. I had fought so hard and come too far.

The door swung open, and Jack stood in the doorway. His eyes widened at the sight of me.

"What the hell?" He looked behind him and then quickly shut the door.

"Jack. Thank God." I sighed with relief. "Please, help me. I can't move with this silver on me. Dr. Kramer locked me in here and secured me with silver. He thinks because tonight is a full moon, I'm going to be powerless and show my true self to everyone here."

"Does it hurt?" He reached for the silver chain at my wrist.

"No. But it's draining my energy. I'm so very tired." A tear slipped down my face.

He wiped it away. "So the silver doesn't hurt? Weird, I always thought it would hurt."

"No. Now please take the chains off me."

His expression changed. "I will, but first, you owe me a kiss." He placed his hands on either side of my face and leaned down. He covered my lips with his.

This kiss was like the last one he'd given me. But this time, it was much more urgent and aggressive. Instead of making me feel desired, it made me feel afraid and trapped.

I tried to turn my face away and break the kiss, but I was too weak.

"Jack—" I couldn't speak more because he shoved his tongue down my throat.

Any attraction I had for him was now replaced by repulsion and fear.

He finally pulled back enough that I could look him in the eyes.

"Jack, what's wrong with your eyes?" His eyes were glowing yellow. They were the eyes of a monster.

"I don't know what you mean. All I know is I want to be inside you now." He shoved handfuls of my dress up to my thighs then fumbled for his belt.

"No." I tried to struggle. "Get off me, you asshole."

Then the door swung open.

A thunderous roar rocked the boat. I wasn't sure if it was in my mind or if it had actually happened. Jack didn't stop trying to get his pants down. I looked at the doorway, and standing there looking ready to kill, was Khalan.

"Get the fuck off her," he roared and stormed towards the bed. He grabbed Jack by the back of his shirt and flung him across the room. He landed with a thud against the wall and slid to the floor.

Khalan didn't wait for Jack to get his feet under him. He was on the werewolf in a second. He grabbed him by the neck and proceeded to pummel him in the face with his large fists. Blood spurted from Jack's broken nose and stained his white shirt.

"Khalan. Stop." I managed to breathe out the words. I wasn't sure he could hear me, though. I was quickly fading into that space I knew there would be no coming back from.

"Rachel." Khalan dropped Jack, who crumpled to the floor. He hurried to the bed. "Are you okay?"

"I will be once this silver is off me." Tears continued sliding down my face. I had never been so happy to see anyone in my life.

"Hang on." He grabbed a pillow and ripped the pillowcase off. He wrapped his hand in the fabric and then reached for the silver chains.

Slowly, he lifted the chains off me and dropped them to the floor.

He freed my hands.

"You should close that door. I don't want anyone to see this and start asking questions." I tried to sit up but was still too weak.

Khalan grabbed Jack by the back of the neck and threw him out of the room onto the deck. "If you ever so much as look at her again, I will fucking kill you." He slammed the door and turned the lock.

Our gazes locked across the room. I tried sitting up, but my trembling body wouldn't support me.

He wrapped the pillowcase over his hand again and unchained my legs from the silver.

He tossed the bonds into a pile in the corner of the room and sat on the bed beside me. He brushed the hair out of my eyes. "Really, are you okay?"

"I'm just weak." My words came out shaken and unsure. Exactly as I felt. "Khalan, don't leave me."

I saw the look of surprise in his eyes. "I will never leave you." He cupped my cheek.

I leaned into his touch. I had just enough strength to lift my hand to his thigh.

"I knew Jack was an asshole, but I didn't know he would chain you to take advantage of you." Khalan growled.

"He didn't chain me. Dr. Kramer did."

"He what?" Khalan blinked.

"He told me that he knew I was a vampire. And because of the full moon tonight, he was going to chain me with silver in order to force me to show my true nature to the world. He was going to use that to help get Cal off the murder charge."

"What a fucking idiot." Khalan stood. "I'm going to make sure he is taken care of once and for all."

"Wait. Don't leave me." I reached for him.

His expression softened, and he sat back down on the bed. "You need to rest. You need to regain your strength."

"I want to sit up."

He cradled me in his arms and lifted me into a seated position. His scent made my heart throb in my chest. I pressed my face into his shirt and rested my hand against him.

"I think I'm messing up your tux with my makeup."

He let out a soft laugh. "I don't care. I borrowed it."

"Borrowed it? I didn't know you had any friends in Charming."

"I don't. I glamoured some schmuck into giving me his." He shrugged. "I think he was contestant number fourteen for this charity event."

"Oddly enough, I don't have a smartass comeback for that. Khalan, I'm glad you're here." I looked up at him.

He was staring down at me, those dark and dangerous eyes locked on my very soul.

"I didn't know that silver would hurt me."

"Normally, it doesn't. Unless you get staked by it." He looked over at the chains. "I smelled something odd on the metal. A weird odor I haven't smelled in centuries."

"Do you know what it is?"

"No, not off the top of my head, but I think they rubbed the silver with it to make you weak."

"Is there any kind of liquid that could do that?" I was feeling energy return to my body, but I wasn't ready to leave Khalan's embrace just yet.

"Not a liquid but…." He stilled and looked at the door.

"What?"

"I need to find Jack. I think he might have had something to do with Dr. Kramer locking you in here."

"But…"

"But nothing, Rachel. He could have raped you."

I shuddered against him and buried my face in his chest again. That wasn't something I wanted to think about.

He tightened his hold on me and pressed a kiss to the top of my head. "As much as I want to stay here with you like this. I have to go take care of Jack."

"What about Dr. Kramer? He's a threat, too." I looked up at him.

He cupped my cheek. "Dr. Kramer is a maniac. Everyone knows that. No one will believe anything he says, including you being a vampire." His thumb rubbed my bottom lip.

My initial attraction to Jack had been nowhere near as strong as what I was feeling for Khalan.

I knew without a doubt that if circumstances were different, I would have taken off my clothes and had sex with Khalan right on this bed. From the groan he let out, and the darkening of his eyes, he felt the same.

"This is not over. This thing between you and me." He stood.

"It better not be. I'm getting tired of waiting." I eased my legs over the side of the bed, and he took my hand. He pulled me up beside him.

"You shouldn't be wearing that dress tonight."

My heart fell. "I paid a lot of money for this dress. I

wanted to look special tonight. I wanted to be desired, just for one night." I turned towards the door, but he caught me around my waist and pulled me against him.

"That's not what I meant," he whispered near my ear.

I shivered at his touch and felt my eyes drift shut. "What did you mean?" My voice sounded husky to my own ears.

"You shouldn't have worn that dress tonight because ever since you walked in, every man in the room—as well as some of the women—have wanted to take you to bed."

"You are the only one who accomplished the task." My heart hammered in my chest this time, not with fear but desire.

He spun me around in his arms until we were face-to-face. He slid his hand down to my waist and pressed my body against his. I gasped at the sensation of his erection pressing into my stomach.

"Like I said, we are not finished here." He slammed his mouth down across mine. I opened my lips under his, and his tongue snaked inside my mouth. I arched against him, wrapping my arms around his neck while kissing him with abandon, a feeling I had never experienced before.

He lifted me up, and I wanted so badly to wrap my legs around him, but my dress was too tight for that.

He reluctantly broke the kiss. I groaned in protest.

"You need to take my blood to get your full strength back." He bit his wrist and held it out to me.

I didn't argue. I sucked. His sweet blood spilled into my mouth, and I moaned like it was dessert.

I reached down with my free hand and caressed his erection.

"Fuck," he moaned.

The last thing either of us wanted to do was leave the room. We wanted to stay, closed away, separated from the world, where we could make love until we were exhausted by pleasure.

I finally pulled my mouth away from him and licked the puncture wounds on his arm.

He bent his head and kissed me. This time, the kiss was soft and gentle.

"You look like a vision tonight," he murmured.

"Thank you. And you look hot."

He gave me a lopsided grin that, had we been in my bedroom, would have melted my panties right off.

"What are we going to do?" I looked at the door.

"You go back to the gambling room. Try to look as if you're having a good time. And when Dr. Kramer sees you, he will know you are not a vampire."

"And you?"

"I'm going to find Jack," he growled.

"Be careful. He knows what to use to weaken us." I pressed my hand to his chest.

"I always am." He kissed my fingertips.

Holding my hand, he walked over to the door and unlocked it. He opened it and looked out. When he felt that it was safe, he let me exit.

He escorted me to the gambling room and then left to find Jack.

CHAPTER 29

*K*halan's blood had revived me to the point I felt invincible. I looked around the room but didn't see any sign of either Jack or Dr. Kramer. Reluctantly, I eased into a seat at one of the blackjack tables.

"Would you like to buy some chips?" The young female dealer smiled politely.

"Sure. I opened my clutch and pulled out a hundred-dollar bill. I wasn't much on gambling. I would much rather spend my money on tangible things.

She smiled and slid some colorful chips my way.

"You like blackjack?" The older man to my right smiled. He was in his late fifties, with graying hair and nice eyes. He looked like someone's grandfather.

"I'm not much of a gambler."

"Of course, you are. I mean, you're here tonight."

"Yes, but for the dating part of it."

"But isn't that what dating is? A gamble? Lord knows who you will end up with. Statistically speaking, there's a one in fifty chance that someone aboard is either a felon, a rapist, or a serial killer."

I looked at him, and my mouth dropped.

"George, don't scare the young lady." An older woman seated on the other side of me patted my arm. She was wearing a sequined black dress and was draped in diamonds. She adjusted her tennis bracelet and then took the cards the dealer handed us. "Don't you mind him. George is a retired police officer."

"Is that so?" I looked at him.

"Guilty as charged. My wife left me ten years ago because she said I was married to my work and not her. Now that I'm retired with a great retirement package, I'm looking for someone to share my life with." He rifled through his cards. "What's your story?"

"I'm divorced with two girls." I picked up my cards and examined my hand.

"Job?"

"Not really. Although I consider being a mom a full-time position."

"You must have gotten a pretty penny in the divorce." The woman gave me a wink. "That's how you do it. When they do wrong, they got to pay. My name is Edna, by the way."

"How do you know the divorce was her idea?" George huffed. "You know, statistics say…"

"Oh, stuff your statistics," Edna groused. "Just look at her. Who in their right mind would divorce someone who looks like that?"

George stopped examining his cards and started examining me. "Did you cheat?"

"Absolutely not." I glared.

"You beat him?"

"I wish I had," I retorted.

"Are you a lesbian?" George brightened.

"No." I gritted my teeth and had the dealer hit me with another card. I sighed when I busted.

"See. I know quality, and you my dear, are quality." Edna nodded appreciatively. "Although in my younger years, I would have given you some competition."

"I'm sure you would have." I smiled at her compliment. "What do you do, Edna?"

"Me? Oh, I marry wealthy men. It's something I've always done. I've outlived three husbands, and I'm on the lookout for husband number four. That's why I'm here."

"Ugh. No one will date you, knowing you are only after them for their money." George scowled.

"They will when they see my bank account. You see, I'm looking for love this time."

"But how will you know if he really loves you and isn't just after you for *your* money?" I looked at her. The thought of someone marrying Edna just for financial gain made me worry for the older woman.

"Honey, here's what I know. Love isn't diamonds or fancy cars. Love is taking care of someone when they are sick, loving them at their worst, and fighting for them when they are at their weakest. If you find a man like that, then you hold onto him. He's a keeper." Edna winked and then hit blackjack.

"Thanks for the advice." I scooped up my remaining chips and stood.

"Leaving already?" George scowled.

"Yes. Blackjack isn't my game."

"Go to the roulette table. You'll have better chances there." George lifted his glass of whiskey to me in farewell.

CHAPTER 30

$\mathcal{I}$ spotted the roulette table and made my way over.

"Were you not going to say hi?" Miles grabbed my elbow.

I glared at him. "Hi, Miles. I wasn't aware you were here." I had been too busy being silvered in a bed to notice.

He released his hold and let his gaze wander down my body.

I cringed.

"You look nice." He forced out the words.

"I look drop-dead gorgeous. You just can't admit it." I smirked and grabbed a glass of champagne from a passing waiter. I ignored Miles and took a sip.

"You're right. You do look beautiful," Miles admitted. He looked around the room and then back at me. "I dare say that people would think we are the most beautiful couple in the room tonight."

"Your ego is astounding. Have you seen the other men on this boat?"

"Yeah, and half of them have one foot on a banana peel and the other in the grave." He snorted.

"Rachel."

I spun around at the sound of Dr. Kramer's voice.

I narrowed my eyes at the vile man.

"What are you…? But I don't understand…" he sputtered.

"Don't understand what? Why don't you clarify?" I arched a brow.

"You were supposed to be drained by the silver." He shook his head, and his eyes bulged.

"You should be turning by now."

"Rachel, who is this little man?" Miles lifted his chin and stepped closer to me. "He's not making any sense."

"He never does," I admitted.

Dr. Kramer jerked his head over at Miles. "Miles Jones?"

"That's *Doctor* Jones to you." Miles sucked back the bourbon in his glass and waved over a server to retrieve him another. "Who are you?"

"Dr. Kramer." He waved his hands animatedly. "I don't understand why the silver and moon aren't working on you." He looked at me.

"What exactly are you a doctor of?" Miles cocked his head.

"He's Cal's psychiatrist."

"That makes a whole lot of fucking sense." Miles snorted.

Dr. Kramer stepped into Miles' personal space. "You won't be laughing when I show the world what she is."

"And what is she?"

"She's a succubus, a legend of old. A vampire," Dr. Kramer yelled.

My heart dropped to the bottom of my stomach, and I forgot to breathe. It was like I was suddenly in a vacuum, and there was no sound.

Everyone in the room turned and looked at us.

Miles looked from Dr. Kramer and then back to me.

"A vampire?" He grabbed the bourbon from the waiter and took a sip. "Well, she did drain me dry in the divorce."

"I did not. You absolutely agreed to the terms. Besides, you are driving a luxury car and are living it up at the penthouse."

A big smile broke out across his face. "I was meaning to tell you, I bought some land, and I'm going to build a new house. State-of-the-art."

"What?" I had never wanted to strangle someone as much as I wanted to strangle Miles. "If you can afford to build a new house, then you can bring Arianna's golf clubs back. And maybe start paying me alimony again." I poked him in the chest.

"Rachel, don't start." Miles sighed.

Dr. Kramer started jumping up and down. "Aren't you paying attention to what I'm saying? I said she's a vampire. Just look how young she looks for her age."

Edna walked up and snorted. "That's called Botox, you fool. And how did you manage to get on this boat anyway? This is for the elite of the South. And from your accent, you don't exactly fall into that category."

A gentle rumble of laughter floated around the room.

I grinned at Edna. She was my kind of woman.

Dr. Kramer pulled a knife out of his jacket pocket. Everyone gasped.

He waved it around the room. "I'll prove it. I'll cut her, and she will drop her fangs and lunge for my neck."

"Ew. As if." The thought of drinking this psycho's blood was as enticing as finding a cockroach in my potato chips.

"Look here. You just need to calm down." Miles held out his hands in defense. He spoke low and slow as if he were talking to an irrational person. Which, he was.

"Dude, you need to put that away." Earl from the limo

stepped up and assessed the situation. He wore a smile, but I could tell he was unnerved by what was happening.

Two security guards walked through the door and looked over at us. I took a step back, and Dr. Kramer took a step closer.

"Easy, buddy. You need to put that away before someone gets hurt." One of the security guards walked over to us.

Dr. Kramer waved his knife around like a crazy person. "You'll believe me when I cut her throat. You'll all understand. It has been foretold that she will reemerge under the full moon to her supernatural strength. You will all thank me for this." He turned to me and lunged.

I tried to step out of the way, but my heel got caught on the rug, and I fell to the floor in a heap.

Dr. Kramer jumped and landed on top of me. Everyone in the room screamed. I heard Miles yell for someone to help, yet I noticed he was too much of a pussy to try and help me himself.

Typical.

I tried to buck the doctor off me, but he was too heavy. My eyes widened as he brought the knife close to my face.

He leaned in close. "That drink you just had was laced with wolfsbane. After it weakens a vampire, it makes them deathly ill. So, once I cut your throat, you'd better heal quickly, or you won't be long for this world. You will be forced to drop your fangs and drink my blood. Once you do that, you will expose yourself to the world." He brought the knife down towards my neck. I raised my arm to block him.

The metallic bite of the knife across my skin had me crying out in pain. I cradled my arm to my chest.

Dr. Kramer lifted the knife high in the air to bring it back down to my neck.

Time slowed.

The screams in the room melted and muddled together

into a white, high-pitched noise. Women in cocktail dresses ran from the room, men yelled for someone to call 911. The musty smell of the rug I was lying on reminded me of my old childhood home and carried with it an unfamiliar fear. The lights above me seemed to dim like a solar eclipse, and I took it as a sign that I was dying.

Indescribable sadness choked me as I thought about my two beautiful girls...and Khalan. I would never have the chance to say goodbye to any of them.

Hot tears slid down my face. I looked up into the face of an evil man who was going to cut my throat in order to expose me as a vampire. He was going to prove a point even at the expense of my death.

It was so fucking unfair.

An animalistic growl echoed in the room. The lights went out, and I was surrounded by darkness.

I closed my eyes and waited for Dr. Kramer to slit my throat. I waited for my blood to spill across my ridiculously expensive dress and onto the riverboat floor. I waited to smell the scent of my death.

"Get the fuck off her!"

The weight of Dr. Kramer on top of me was suddenly gone. I heard the thud of punches being meted out and bones breaking under fists.

Suddenly, hands were underneath me, lifting me into the air. I saw the dim light of the Memphis area as I was carried outside onto the deck of the boat.

"Khalan?" I looked up at him.

"You'll be okay. I promise." His eyes bore into mine.

"Oh my God! Is she okay?" Gina hurried over. She grabbed my uninjured arm and held my hand. "She needs a doctor."

"Then call her ex-husband over here," Khalan ordered.

I looked up at him. "Will your blood not heal me?"

"Yes. But it's going to look odd. I need that bastard to at least tend to you on the boat."

I rested my head against his chest. "Khalan, I think that knife had wolfsbane on it, as did the drink I had—at least according to the psycho."

His eyes widened in horror. "Fuck."

"Am I going to die?"

"No. But you will feel really shitty for a while." He walked over to the open deck and knelt with me in his arms.

I pressed my hand to his chest. "Does this feel familiar? You carrying me back to your house after I was beheaded?"

"*Almost* beheaded," he corrected. He brushed the hair out of my face. "And, yes, it does. Once again, you have on a beautiful outfit."

I laughed weakly. "I wasn't wearing anything but a bow the first time you saw me."

"I know." He tried to give me a smirk, but I could see the fear behind his eyes.

"I'm dying, aren't I?" I reached up and touched his cheek. "Promise me something."

"What?"

"Promise me that you will look after Gabby and Arianna."

"Rachel…"

"Khalan, I need to know that you will be there for them when I'm gone."

"Stop being dramatic. You aren't going anywhere. I won't let that happen." His voice grew husky, and I knew he was trying to put on a brave face.

"Khalan. I do have one regret."

"What? Becoming a vampire?"

"No. I regret not being with you."

"You're always with me."

"No. I regret not making love with you. I've lived my life worried about what other people think of me and letting that

161

guide my decisions. If I could do it over, I would live on my terms and do what makes me happy."

"Rachel, I'm not going to let you die." He leaned down and pressed his lips to mine. The kiss was gentle and soft, so unlike my Maker's personality.

"Rachel?" Miles knelt beside me. He cut his eyes at Khalan.

"You need to take care of her arm," Khalan ordered.

"But she needs stitches, and I don't have those supplies with me at the moment."

"There's a first-aid kit in the wheelhouse. It should be extensive," Gina said over Miles' shoulder.

"I'll go see." Miles gave Khalan a hard look and then hurried away.

"How is she?" Gina looked at Khalan.

"She'll be okay. But I don't want everyone coming over here gawking." Khalan glared.

"They won't. I ordered security to keep everyone away." Gina nodded. "Good thing you were here, Mr…"

"Astor. Khalan Astor."

"Oh, well…" Her eyes widened. "Are you related to—?"

"We are in luck. They have sutures." Miles knelt beside me. He opened the box and rifled through the contents.

"I need her flat." He looked at Khalan.

"No. You will sew her arm up while she is in my arms. I will not put her down." Khalan narrowed his eyes.

"But…"

"But nothing, you asshole. You will sew her up while I hold her." Khalan tightened his grip on me.

Miles gave Khalan a stern look but nodded. He proceeded to prepare my arm. Miles pulled out the needle and suture.

I grimaced.

"Keep your eyes on me," Khalan commanded.

I looked up at him. His dark eyes held mine captive. He stroked the side of my cheek with his palm.

I hissed at the sting of the needle.

"Easy," Khalan growled.

"I'm sorry, but I don't have anything to numb the area," Miles said.

"It's okay. Keep going." I looked at Khalan and held up my arm for Miles to sew.

Khalan held my gaze and seemed to take on my pain as I was being stitched up. Oddly enough, I didn't feel any stronger. I still felt weak. It must be the wolfsbane.

"I'm done." Miles cut the suture. "But she's going to need to go to the ER to get a tetanus shot."

"I'll take her once we dock."

"I'll have the ambulance waiting for us once we arrive," Gina offered.

"I said, I will take her. I don't trust anyone else to look after her." Khalan growled.

"I'm sorry, but do you know my wife?" Miles spat out.

"*Ex*-wife," I corrected.

Miles lifted his chin in defiance.

"I do know Rachel. And you and I have met before, but you obviously have your head so far up your ass that you don't remember. You seem to be that kind of man." Khalan scoffed.

"What kind of man?" Miles asked.

"The kind who only thinks about himself. The kind who didn't bother to put himself in front of Rachel when that asshole was coming at her with a knife. The kind who needs his ass kicked all the way back to Charming." Khalan's eyes were glowing with hatred.

Gina snorted and patted Khalan on the back. "I don't know who you are exactly, sir, but I, for one, am sure glad you're here." She tugged on Miles' arm. "Come on. You are no longer needed here."

Miles glared and stormed away, his ego clearly hurt.

Gina winked at me. "I think he's a keeper, Rachel." She stood and headed over to reassure the rest of the people on board that the emergency was over.

"How are you feeling?"

"Woozy." I placed my hand on my stomach.

"It's the wolfsbane. You've had my blood, so the effects of the drug should be wearing off."

"I'm not sure that's why I'm woozy." Khalan lifted me and carried me across the way to a sitting area near a window. I could feel everyone's eyes on me as he strode across the room.

"Everyone is looking at us."

"I'm sure they're looking at you." The muscle in his cheek flexed. "Every male on this boat wishes he had you for himself."

I tightened my arms around his neck. "Every male?" My heart hammered in my chest.

He stopped and gently set me on the loveseat. He knelt at my feet as he straightened my dress. He looked up at me. "Yes."

"Khalan?"

His pupils dilated, and he pressed his hands on either side of my thighs. He leaned in close, and I thought I was going to hyperventilate from the anticipation of what he was going to do.

I looked into his eyes. They were dark and dangerous, and I found myself wanting to be alone with him.

"Yes, Rachel, every male." His mouth was so close to mine, yet he didn't kiss me.

For years, I'd always tried to do the right thing. I'd been taught from the foster system to be good, to keep my head down. I'd let Miles mold me into the perfect housewife, who supported her husband no matter what. I'd covered up my pain and desires under the mask of happiness when I had been with my friends. For years, I'd tried to keep up appearances so people wouldn't talk about me, or so they'd want to be my friend.

In the end, it hadn't stopped Miles from cheating or kept my best friend from betraying me. It had not made me any happier.

I could feel everyone in the room, staring at me from a distance. I could feel their desire for me and their hatred of me.

To them, I was a tarnished woman who might have deserved getting cheated on. Hell, for all I knew, they were all secretly glad it was me who'd gone through hell. People did tend to have a mindset of *'at least it didn't happen to me.'*"

In that moment, everyone and everything fell away. In that moment, it was just Khalan and me in that room on the riverboat. And in that moment, it was only his scent and his hot breath across my lips.

In that moment, nothing else mattered.

I reached up and touched his cheek. He leaned into my palm. "You realize people are watching."

"What people?" I rubbed my thumb across his cheek.

"Rachel." His voice was a deep warning, which made me want him even more. "There will be talk."

"I don't give a fuck." I meant it. "I want what I want."

He growled and moved a fraction of an inch, which seemed like lightyears away, and covered my lips with his.

I opened my mouth under his. His tongue claimed mine with an intensity I had never experienced before. I wrapped my hands around the back of his neck, pulling him closer.

His body pressed against mine, and I could feel his desire for me pressing into my stomach.

I wanted to open my legs, but my damn dress was too tight.

He broke the kiss, and I moaned in protest.

"What I want to do to you is not for everyone's eyes." He lowered his voice.

"Whatever that is, I'm up for it." I tried to bring his mouth back to mine, but he grabbed my hand and kissed it.

"Remember, your arm is supposed to be hurt." He gave me a knowing look.

I sighed.

"And we are almost at the dock, so we are getting off. Now." He stood and then bent down and scooped me up in his arms.

"Are you sure you don't want the ambulance to...?" Gina rushed over to us.

"Yes. I'm sure," Khalan growled.

Gina looked at me. "Rachel, I know this night has not turned out like I promised."

"You're right. It turned out even better." I smiled and snuggled into Khalan's large chest.

Gina blushed and ducked her head. "I think I'll go find my husband."

Khalan strode across the room. The crowd parted for him. I closed my eyes, not caring about what the gossip mill would be talking about in the morning, and wished that we had the rest of the night alone.

"The gangplank is engaged, sir."

I opened my eyes.

"Thank you." Khalan nodded and began the descent to dry land. When we reached the bottom, the police were waiting.

"Is she okay?" one of the cops asked.

"She will be." Khalan nodded and kept walking.

I looked over his shoulder as the police boarded the riverboat. The guests had quickly forgotten about me and were now focused on the cops. That was a good thing.

"We're almost to the car. I had to park all the way by that building. The lots were all filled by the time I got here." Khalan glanced at me.

"I can walk, Khalan."

"No. I'm carrying you." He stopped when we rounded the corner of the building.

I looked over at the sleek white sports car. "Is that yours?"

He didn't take his eyes off me. "I couldn't very well show up on my Harley, could I?"

I grinned. "You could have, but you would have wrinkled your tux." I slid my hand down his chest. "Nice tux, by the way."

"Thank you." He gently placed my feet on the ground and slid his hand up my thigh to rest on my waist. He glanced down and then looked back up at me. "You have some blood on your gown."

"Perfect." I grimaced. "What a waste of money. I'm not even going to tell you how much I spent on this stupid dress."

"It's not wasted. You walked in there tonight like the badass woman you are. If it showed you how beautiful and strong you are, then the money was well spent."

I licked the corner of my mouth.

"Don't do that." His voice was thick and hoarse.

"Do what?" I blinked.

"Do that thing with your tongue. It makes me want to do really bad things. Things that shouldn't be done in public." He leaned in and brushed his face against the crook of my neck.

I moaned. I wanted so much more from him.

"Don't do that." I rested my hand on his chest. The play of his muscles under my hand was driving me insane.

"You shouldn't be doing that. You must be under her spell."

The hair on the back of my neck stood at attention. I jerked my head around and saw Dr. Kramer standing there, bloodied and beaten, but standing there nonetheless.

"The police… They let you go?" I stepped back into Khalan's chest. He wrapped his hand around my waist and gently shoved me behind him to shield me from the madman.

"They didn't find me." Dr. Kramer narrowed his eyes. "Do you think you are just going to get away with being what you are? Do you think there are no consequences to being a killer?"

"I'm not a killer, you psycho," I screamed into the night.

"There's no one here that will hear you. They are all too busy with what's going on on the riverboat. Besides, the sirens will drown you out."

"Rachel, go get in my car," Khalan thundered.

"What? I'm not leaving you here with this lunatic." I clutched his sleeve.

"I said, get in the fucking car," Khalan growled. "I'm going to handle him once and for all."

"See, you've glamoured another sucker into doing your bidding." Dr. Kramer's eyes shone with malice. He reached into his tattered suit and pulled out a cross. "I am going to send you back to the pit of Hell from whence you came.'"

"Hell would be me being married to my ex-husband. So, nope, not going back there." I narrowed my eyes. I leaned over to Khalan. "Does he know that crosses don't affect us?"

"No. He's an idiot. A very dangerous one that I'm tired of hearing from." Khalan glanced at me. "Get in the car."

"No." I crossed my arms. "If you are going to do battle with Van Helsing here, I am, too."

"Dr. Kramer isn't who he says he is." Jack appeared out of

the shadows. Gone was his jacket, and his white shirt was covered in blood.

"Jack! How did Dr. Kramer get off the boat? I thought you had him cornered." I narrowed my eyes.

"I did. Until he shot me with this." Jack held up a silver bullet. "I dug it out before it could poison me."

"So, he knows..."

"He knows I'm a werewolf," Jack admitted. "That's because when we were outside, the full moon caused my eyes to change to yellow."

"And yellow eyes mean what?"

"Bloodlust," Khalan stated.

"So now he's going to kill you, too, Jack." I sighed. Could no one around Charming keep their mouths shut?

"No, he won't." Jack gave me a grim smile. "He wouldn't kill his own."

"Wait. What?" I looked from Jack back to Dr. Kramer.

"That's right. I'm a werewolf. And I've had to fight your kind all my life. Vampires have taken from me, and I'm not taking it anymore."

"What did they take from you?" I wondered if maybe someone had drained his pet dog or hamster.

"Oh, shut up, Kramer. No one likes a bitter old wolf." Jack looked down at his bloody shirt. "There's no way I'm getting all this blood out."

"I will have my vengeance. On the death of Samantha."

"Who the fuck is Samantha?" Jack looked from the doctor to me.

"The girl that Cal killed," Khalan offered.

"Then do your job. Cal is the one who killed her. You shouldn't be protecting him." I wanted to stomp my foot, but something about the way Dr. Kramer was looking at me had fear clawing its way up my throat.

"Samantha was mine." Dr. Kramer pulled out a wooden stake.

"Yours?" I grimaced. "Aren't you a little old...?"

"Shut your filthy mouth," Kramer thundered. "She was mine until Cal took her away. He never would have had her if he had not been glamoured."

"You fool. Samantha used Cal, like she used you. For money. She was a sugarbaby." Khalan cocked his head. "Cal was willing to pay more than you, so she started seeing him regularly. That pissed you off, and now you're trying to blame someone else for your problems. Grow some balls and get over it."

"What's a sugarbaby?" I looked at the men.

"Someone who exchanges favors for money." Khalan kept his gaze trained on Dr. Kramer.

"I thought that was called a hooker." I frowned.

"Sometimes, the favors aren't sexual. Sometimes, it involves traveling or dinner or just spending time with them." Jack shrugged.

"And this is a thing?" Why the hell had I not heard of this before?

"Yes, and don't even think about doing it," Khalan growled.

"Like I would even have time." I crossed my arms and glared.

"Prepare to meet your final death." Dr. Kramer grinned maniacally.

"That cross isn't going to hurt me, and I can take that stupid stake out of your hand before you blink, asshole." I uncrossed my arms. I was so done with this shit tonight.

"Really?" Dr. Kramer unbuttoned his suit and opened up his jacket. There were wires and something that looked like playdough, and a timer strapped to his body.

"Fuck. It's a bomb." Jack's eyes widened.

"Not just a bomb. It's filled with silver. Once this goes off, the shrapnel will impale anyone within a fifty-foot radius. I'm not afraid of death, are you, Rachel Jones?"

I was, actually. I wasn't sure where I would end up. When I was human, I was sure I was going to Heaven, but now as a vampire, I wasn't sure what the requirements were. Did vampires even get past the pearly gates? Did we go to Hell? Or were we bound to walk eternity in solitude?

"I have children," I pleaded.

"They will be better off without you. You are nothing but a monster."

Khalan growled. I could smell his hatred coming off him in waves. I pressed farther away from Dr. Kramer and the danger.

"Rachel, I want you to run as fast and as far as you can." Khalan kept his gaze on Kramer as he spoke to me.

"But I'm not leaving you here."

"Yes. You are."

"Khalan…"

Khalan turned and looked at me. His eyes were both hard and sad. "As your Maker, I command you to run."

Fear flooded my body. I didn't want to leave him. But I had no control over my body now. My feet began to move, and suddenly, I found myself running.

My heels hurt my feet as I ran. Tears streamed down my face, but I couldn't stop myself from running.

I'd left him. I'd left Khalan to die in my place.

I made it to the river's edge. A loud explosion broke the stillness of the night. I turned around. A big, orange, angry ball of fire billowed up into the night sky.

I waited for an eternity to see Khalan walk out of that fire and back to me.

He didn't.

I started walking in that direction. I needed to see for myself.

"Ma'am, it's not safe." An officer grabbed my arm. "We've got fire trucks on the way."

I screamed and crumpled to the ground. The rocks bit into my knees, but I didn't mind. The pain around my heart hurt worse. I buried my head in hands and wept.

"Rachel!" Gina's heels clacked on the asphalt. She knelt beside me. "Oh, my God. Are you okay? Did you get knocked down by that explosion? And you shouldn't be out here by yourself, the cops said that psycho who attacked you somehow got off the boat."

"I know," I cried.

"Rachel. I'm getting the paramedics."

"No. I'm not hurt. I'm just…."

"I know, honey. Mentally exhausted. After everything that happened tonight." Gina eased onto the ground beside me. She wrapped her arms around my shoulders and pulled me in for a hug. I was too tired to fight her.

The fire truck sirens screeched into the night. Finally, Gina let me go. "We need to get up from here. We are going to ruin these dresses."

"I don't care." I reluctantly got up from the ground, my heart broken.

"Where is your man?" She looked around. "Never mind. I'll find you a ride home. I'm going to be here all night filling out police reports and doing damage control."

I didn't bother answering her. Edna found me outside and offered to take me home.

I numbly got into her Mercedes and mumbled my address. She plugged it into her GPS, and we drove away from Memphis, headed back to Charming.

CHAPTER 31

"*A*re you sure you don't want me to come in with you, dear? I could fix you something to drink to help settle your nerves." Edna patted my hand.

"No." I was numb inside. I didn't want to be around anyone. "Thank you for the ride home."

She nodded. "You know, I once had a man that looked at me like that tall fellow looked at you tonight. I let him go because I thought I needed someone who could provide me with financial security instead of following my heart." She shook her head. "I was a fool."

I swallowed the lump in my throat.

"I didn't see him when we left. I was sure he was going to take you home tonight." She gave me a wink.

"He's gone." It hurt to say the words. Hot tears slid down my face. Just when I thought I couldn't cry anymore, I still had tears left in my soul.

"I wouldn't be so sure." She patted my hand. "If you two had a fight, I'm sure you can fix it. Don't let him go. I know a good man when I see one. That one is a good man."

She thought Khalan was alive. She didn't know. How

173

could she? After the explosion, the fire trucks had descended on the scene and fought the flames. They were still trying to put out the fire when we left.

I'd overheard the fire chief say that there were two dead bodies and a whole lot of ash.

The ash. Khalan. It had to be.

He'd told me that after we'd killed Memphis and beheaded her, she would turn to ash if the fire got hot enough. In her case, the fire trucks had gotten to her tour bus and put out the flames before the fire could decimate her body.

But Khalan had died in an explosion caused by a bomb. There was no way he could have survived.

And neither had Jack.

"Thanks again for the ride." I opened the door and slid out of the car. I couldn't stand to be around anyone right now.

I wanted to get inside my home and lock myself away from the world.

I hurried up to my front door. I fumbled with the key before finally getting it into the lock. I opened the door and locked it behind me.

"Mommy?" Gabby came out of the kitchen with a bowl of ice cream. "What happened? You look like you've been dragged through the mud."

The girls. I had completely forgotten about them being home.

I wiped my face and forced a grin. "It felt about like that."

"Arianna, come here," Gabby called over her shoulder.

Arianna came to a stop when she saw me. "Oh my gosh. Are you okay? Why is your arm bandaged?"

The bandage. I had completely forgotten about it.

I ripped it off. My cut was healed, and the stitches had

fallen out. I wadded up the gauze in my hand. "It was nothing. A scrape." I shook my head.

"Your dress. Mom, your dress is ruined." Arianna's eyes widened.

"I know. It wasn't a...not a good night." I tried very hard to hold in my tears, but they couldn't be contained. They spilled out of my eyes and ran down my cheeks.

"What's wrong?" Arianna hurried over to me as I slid to the floor.

"He's gone."

"Who?" Arianna's eyes widened. "Daddy? Did something happen to Daddy?"

"No. He's fine." I wiped my tears with the back of my hand. "It's Khalan."

"What happened?" Arianna held my hand between hers. Gabby sat on the other side of me.

"I don't want to talk about it." I dried my tears and gave my girls watery smiles.

"You really liked him, didn't you?" Gabby cocked her head.

I looked at her and then Arianna. "Yes, sweetie. I really liked him."

"I think you need a warm bath. I'll go run the water and add in your favorite bubbles." Gabby nodded. She hurried to my bathroom. A few seconds later, I heard the water running.

I got to my feet. Gabby returned.

"I'm sorry, girls. I didn't mean to worry you guys." I pulled them close to me and held them.

When I released them, they both looked at me with such compassion, it shook me.

"It's okay, Mom." Arianna nodded. "We just want you to be happy. And we know that Khalan made you happy. Whatever happened between you two, I hope you work it out."

A tear escaped. I shook my head. "I don't think that's going to happen." He was gone. There was no coming back from that.

"Come on. You need to get into the bubble bath before it gets cold." Gabby took my hand and led me to the bathroom. She picked up her bowl of ice cream from where she'd placed it on the counter and held it out to me. "You need this more than me."

They left and closed the door behind them.

I set the bowl down and looked back at the mirror.

My dress was stained with blood and ripped up the side. My hair was a mess, and my makeup had run from my crying.

I was beyond a hot mess.

I stepped out of my heels and slowly peeled the dress from my body. My stomach turned when I looked at the bowl of ice cream, so I left it on the counter to melt.

I dipped my toe into the water and then stepped in. I sank down below the bubbles until everything was covered except my head. My hair was getting wet, but I didn't care.

My heart was broken, and I was swallowed up by guilt.

I should have told Khalan how I felt before tonight.

I'd let my pride and my fear of getting hurt again get in the way.

Now, he was gone.

I cried in my bubbles until the water turned cool. I couldn't stay in the tub forever, but I didn't have the strength to get out.

Unless I was going to live my undead life in cold bathwater, I needed to move.

I stood and grabbed the fluffy towel on the side of the tub. I wrapped it around me and stood at my large bathroom mirror.

"Mom, can you come into the kitchen when you get out?" Arianna knocked on the door.

"Sure. Just give me a minute."

I grabbed a washcloth and scrubbed away the makeup and tears.

I dried my face and threw on some clothes.

I slowly made my way into the kitchen. "Why are you guys still up?" I looked at Arianna and Gabby.

"We wanted to wait up for you and make sure you got home okay." Arianna shrugged.

"And Arianna got scared when she heard something outside." Gabby grinned.

"Shut up." Arianna glared at her sister.

"Well, you did. You wanted to call the cops, but it was just Scooby digging around in the back yard."

I sighed. "Well, I'm home safe and sound, so you guys can go to bed now."

They each hugged me tightly. I didn't want to let them go.

"Thanks, girls." I smiled.

"You know, Mommy, we should really get a dog. They are great for protection. And they're loyal," Gabby said brightly. "We've never had a dog before."

"That's because Dad didn't want it messing up the house." Arianna rolled her eyes.

"Well, he's no longer here. So, I vote for a dog." Gabby raised her hand. Arianna did, too.

"Let's talk about it in the morning." I nodded. "Now, I think everyone needs to go to bed."

They nodded and made their way to their rooms. I flipped the switch on the wall, and the room went dark. I was never tired after dark. But tonight, I was bone-tired. Weary from living in a world of mean and evil people.

Khalan might have been a vampire, but he had more compassion than a lot of humans.

I wrapped the robe tighter around me and headed back to my bedroom.

I shut the door behind me and locked it. I didn't want the girls to walk in on my hysterical crying.

I looked around and tried to regulate my breathing, but it was so stuffy. I ran to the window and opened it. I stuck my head out and sucked in deep breaths.

"Rachel."

I jumped at the sound of my name and hit my head on the window. I turned around. Standing by my bed was Khalan.

He was no longer wearing a tux, but his signature black jeans and black T-shirt stretched to within an inch of its life. His hair wasn't pulled back but hanging around his shoulders.

"Am I dreaming? I must be dreaming," I muttered. I slowly walked towards the figment of my aggrieved imagination.

"You're not dreaming," he said, watching me get closer.

"Khalan?" I stopped inches from him and reached out to touch his face. I collapsed into tears when my fingers caressed his stubbled cheek.

He gathered me in his arms. I clung to him as I cried.

"It's okay. Everything's okay." He scooped me up in his arms and carried me over to the loveseat. He set me on the couch and then sat beside me.

It wasn't close enough. I crawled into his lap and wrapped my arms around his neck and wept.

He held me tight and kissed the top of my head. "Rachel, everything is okay. Please, don't cry."

"Don't cry?" I jerked back and looked at him. "I thought you were dead. I saw the bomb explode. And then the fire-fighters were talking about finding two bodies and a pile of ash." I poked him in his chest. "I thought that pile of ash was you."

He grabbed my fingers and pressed his lips to them. "I know, and I'm sorry, sweetheart. But I couldn't let you stay there with that crazy man. He could have hurt you."

"I don't understand. He said the bomb had silver fragments in it. He said that when it exploded, it would impale me." I looked at his chest and lifted his shirt. His muscled flesh was unharmed. "But you don't have any injuries." I ran my hand down his chest, pretending to check for injuries but really just wanting to feel him up.

"Rachel. You shouldn't do that." His voice was low and dangerous, and I could tell from his dilated pupils that he wanted me.

"Tell me what happened." I pressed my palm to his chest.

He covered my hand with his. "Before I told you to run, I noticed that Kramer had a dead man's trigger. He was willing to die to prove what you are. That's why I told you to run. And when you took off, Jack started running his mouth and telling Kramer that the girl who was killed never loved him. I started to rush Kramer so I could get control of the trigger, but that fucker Jack jumped him and broke his neck. That's when he dropped the detonator, and the bomb exploded."

"But what about the silver?"

"The asshole apparently didn't know his metals well. He clearly got his silver online and didn't check it. It wasn't silver. It was pieces of iron that had been sprayed silver."

"And you found all this out, how?"

"By talking to the police. They didn't know I was over by the bomb when it went off. They knew I had gotten into a fight when Kramer cut you. They said they had searched his house and found a manifesto on his computer for ridding the world of vampires along with bogus vampire sites that boasted about weapons to kill the creatures of the night." He snorted.

"So the iron didn't hurt you? But what about the fire? You

told me fire could kill a vampire and even turn the body to ash if it burned hot enough."

"And that's true. But after the explosion, I dragged myself into the building nearby."

"And Jack?"

He narrowed his eyes. "Jack managed to get away. I saw him dragging a body from the dock where the homeless people camp. I'm sure he wanted me to think he died in the fire."

"What an asshole." I sniffed. "I hope he doesn't come back to Charming."

"I don't think he will, unless he thinks he has a reason." He cocked his head.

"Don't look at me. I hope I never see him again."

His expression softened.

I wrapped my arms around his neck. He buried his face in the crook of my neck and held me close.

I could feel his breath on my neck as he inhaled deeply. It sent tiny shivers of pleasure up and down my body.

I clung to him like a lifeline.

The man I had once thought a monster was now someone I couldn't imagine living without.

Oh, how far we had come.

"You feel so good." He tightened his hold on me. One hand snaked down my back to cup my butt. The other slid up to cradle the back of my head.

I moaned at his touch. I'd had plenty of fantasies about Khalan, but nothing compared to how he made me feel in his arms in real life.

"Don't you dare think about stopping. Not this time." I turned my head. He growled and covered my lips with his.

"Not happening," he murmured against my lips. Then he deepened the kiss, his tongue swiping against mine in a wicked dance.

He tasted hot and spicy. I craved more.

He reached for the hem of my shirt and tugged it over my

head then pulled his off. I gasped at the expanse of muscle. I ran my hands across his chest, running my fingers into each defined crease.

He nuzzled my neck and tugged my bra straps off my shoulders. "Beautiful," he breathed against my skin in between kisses.

I found his mouth and kissed him, tangling my fingers into his hair. His fingers went to the button of my jeans. He tugged them down, and I stepped out of them.

I grabbed his zipper and pulled. He bent and pulled off his jeans.

He wasn't wearing any underwear.

I grasped his large erection and stroked.

His head fell back, and he moaned.

He pulled me into his arms and kissed me while I continued touching him.

His fingers found the clasp of my bra. He pulled it off and tossed it onto the floor. He grabbed my panties and tugged, ripping them to shreds.

Once fully naked, he pressed his naked body into mine and kissed me deeply.

I dug my fingernails into his flesh and arched into him. My body was aching and on fire.

He picked me up, and I wrapped my legs around his waist. I reached between us and guided his erection into my aching body.

He turned and pressed my back against the wall. He thrust hard and fully entered me.

I moaned in ecstasy. His mouth covered mine in a blistering heat.

Our breaths mingled as he thrust inside me, slow and deep. I tightened my fingers in his hair and sucked his tongue into my mouth.

He growled.

He buried his face into the crook of my neck and sucked the sensitive flesh there.

"Don't stop." I dug my nails intro his back.

His thrusts grew faster. I felt my orgasm building. He ground against me, sending me spiraling into the universe on a wave of pleasure.

He growled and bit my neck as he reached his own pleasure.

"That was…" I said breathlessly.

"Amazing," he whispered near my ear.

He trailed kisses across my cheek to my mouth. This time when he kissed me, it was slow and gentle.

He carried me over to my bed and pulled down the covers. He gently placed me on the mattress.

He gazed down at me, lust still evident in his eyes. "You are so beautiful."

He crawled over to me and covered my body.

This time when we made love, it was gentle, and we took our time discovering each other's bodies.

I had never felt more desirable or cherished than when I was in Khalan's arms.

CHAPTER 33

When I woke, I looked across the bed.
Empty. Khalan was gone.

My heart sank. He'd left way before dawn. I had hoped he would linger a little longer.

I forced my feet out of bed and threw my robe over my naked body.

I made my way through the darkness towards my girls' bedrooms.

They had seen me so upset after the charity event. I smiled, thinking back to how kind they had been. I was blessed with great kids.

I stopped at Arianna's room and slowly opened the door.

She was lying on her side, her hands pillowed under her cheek. I leaned against the doorframe and counted her slow, rhythmic breaths.

After a few minutes, I closed the door and headed to Gabby's room.

I reached for the doorknob. A small noise came from behind the closed door.

Fear jumped into my throat. I threw open the door.

A furry head jerked itself in my direction. The dog let out a whimper.

"How did you get in here?" I said to the German Shepherd.

He cocked his head at me like it was a stupid question.

Gabby, still asleep, moaned and turned over.

The dog, who was lying at her feet, turned his attention to her. When she was still, the dog looked back at me.

"You look familiar," I whispered and slowly crept closer to the animal.

He immediately sat up and stuck out his tongue in what appeared to be a goofy grin.

"You're Killer." It was the same dog that Khalan had brought over to *babysit* the girls while we went out one night.

I stuck out my hand. He didn't bother sniffing it but gave me a big lick from wrist to knuckle.

"Ew." I wiped my hand on the sleeve of my robe.

Killer cocked his head and studied me intently.

"Where did you come from?" I glanced at Gabby's window. It was closed and securely locked.

I glanced around the room, and my gaze fell on a folded piece of paper on Gabby's desk.

I walked over and picked up the note. On the outside was written: *For Gabby and Arianna.*

I glanced at Gabby, who was still sound asleep, and then began unfolding the letter.

I walked over to the window. The moon was full, and the light spilled into the room.

I held the missive under the moonlight.

Dear Gabby and Arianna,

I am three years old and a German Shepherd. You can name me whatever you want. I was left behind by my family when they moved, and now I am hoping you will be open to letting me come live with you. I may be big, but I still have a puppy heart. I love playing fetch, chewing on bones (and shoes!), taking naps with my family, and getting scratched on the butt. Things I don't like are mean people (I'm very protective), getting yelled at (I have a sensitive heart), being ignored or left alone, and when my family is upset.

If you let me come live with you, I promise not to pee inside (most days), to protect your family from danger (I have sharp teeth), and most importantly, to love you until I cross the Rainbow Bridge.

Love,

Your new dog

I carefully folded the paper and held it up to my nose. I sniffed.

Khalan. I could smell his scent all over the letter.

He had brought my girls a dog.

I blinked back the tears stinging the backs of my eyes and carefully walked out of the room. I quietly made my way back to my bedroom and stifled a yawn.

I crawled back into bed as dawn approached, my heart warm.

"*M*ommy, wake up!" Gabby bounced on the bed.

I cracked open an eye. Both Gabby and Arianna were sitting on my bed, smiling from ear to ear.

"I'm up, I'm up." I sat up and braced my back against the headboard. "What's up?"

"Look!" Arianna pointed to the floor at the end of the bed.

I crawled over and peered over the footboard. There, sitting patiently, was the German Shepherd. He cocked his head at me.

"He was on my bed when I woke up!" Gabby said. "Come on, Booger." She patted her hand on the bed.

The dog stood and leapt.

"We are not calling him Booger." Arianna shook her head.

"Where did he come from?" I bit my lip to keep from smiling.

"He's a gift." Arianna smiled.

"From who?"

"I have an idea. But I'm not saying." Arianna grinned. "Can we keep him?"

"I don't know, girls. I mean, having a dog is a big responsibility. He needs to be walked and fed and…"

"And he needs a family to love," Gabby added. She hugged the dog and buried her face in his soft fur.

"We can take care of him, we promise. Right, Gabby?" Arianna gave me a hopeful look.

"Yes. You won't have to do anything. We will feed him and walk him and even bathe him," Gabby pleaded.

I reached out and petted the dog. "Well, we'll have to run to the store and get him some dog food."

"No, we won't," Arianna said hopefully. "There's a large bag of kibble by the kitchen door."

"Really?"

"Yes. And that means the person who brought him here already knows we will be a good family for him." She shrugged her shoulders. "Khalan's pretty smart."

"You think Khalan brought him?"

"Yes, don't you? I mean, Dad never let us have a dog. He said they were dirty animals." Arianna narrowed her eyes. "I think we should have Khalan over for dinner tonight. To thank him for Rascal."

"We are not naming him Rascal. That's a stupid name." Gabby glared.

"I think that's a great idea, Arianna."

"The name?" she brightened.

"No, having Khalan over for dinner." I laughed. "But first, let's settle on a name." I tapped my chin with my finger. "How about Karma? I mean, it kind of means destiny."

Both girls smiled.

"Yeah. I like it." Arianna nodded.

"Gabby?" I looked at my youngest.

"Me, too. It fits him." She smiled.

And just like that, we had named our first pet.

We spent the rest of the day outside, playing with Karma.

We bathed him and fed him after getting him acquainted with our home. It was hard to stay awake, but as soon as the sun dipped below the horizon, I was getting my energy back.

"What do you want for dinner?" I asked the girls across the kitchen island. Karma was curled on a blanket by the window, sleeping. I would have to remember to get a dog bed tomorrow.

"Lasagna," Arianna said.

"How does that sound to you, Gabby?"

"Yes!" She hopped off the barstool and padded over to Karma. She lay down and curled up next to him.

I watched as she stroked his fur while he slept.

"Make enough for Khalan." Arianna slid off the stool and moved to sit next to Karma.

It struck me that we had spent the whole day together as a family. And the only time Arianna had her cell phone out was to take pictures of Karma and send them to friends.

I gathered up the ingredients for dinner. While I cooked, the girls roused the dog and took him back to Arianna's room to play.

By the time dinner was ready, I began setting out the plates at the bar.

"Why don't we sit at the dining room table?" Arianna asked.

"Okay." I wasn't going to argue.

I walked into the dining room and began to set the table.

I glanced up at the window and saw a face. I jumped.

"*Khalan. You scared me to death,*" I mouthed the words. "Come in." I motioned with my hand.

I walked over and unlocked the front door.

"This is a first." I shut the door behind him.

"What is?" He scowled.

"You using the front door."

"Khalan! You came for dinner." Gabby ran and threw herself at him. She hugged him around his waist.

Khalan's eyes grew wide, and he looked at me for help.

I grinned and shrugged.

"Arianna, Khalan is here," Gabby screamed.

I turned. Arianna was standing in the doorway of the kitchen with Karma at her side. The dog recognized Khalan and ran to him. He placed his paws on Khalan's large chest and licked him in the face.

Khalan grinned and scratched the dog behind the ears.

We all stood rooted to the spot, watching the interaction.

"Khalan, thank you for Karma," Arianna said quietly.

The dog stopped licking Khalan and looked at Arianna.

"How did you know it was me?" He frowned.

"I just knew." She shrugged. "Come, sit. Mom made lasagna for dinner."

"I just came to talk to your mom," Khalan said.

"Please stay for dinner. We never have any visitors." Gabby tugged on his arm.

"Yeah, stay. Mom's lasagna is really good." Arianna walked over and pulled out a chair. "You can sit here."

"I need to talk to your mom first." He looked at me.

"Arianna and Gabby, can you finish setting the table?"

"Sure." The girls grabbed the napkins and silverware from the dining room table and began placing them around the plates.

Khalan followed me into the kitchen.

"You are staying, right? The girls will be disappointed if you don't." I looked at him. My face heated as I thought about how many times we had made love last night.

I focused on turning off the oven and grabbing some potholders to pull the lasagna out.

"If it's okay." He stood behind me and put his hands on my hips. "Here, let me get that. It's hot." He gently moved me out of the way and put the potholders in his hands. He gently lifted the casserole out of the oven and placed it on top of the range top.

"You realize I don't eat. But I'll make an effort for your girls." His voice was deep but soft.

"Thank you." My body heated at his closeness. The last thing on my mind was eating, but I had the girls to think of.

"I'll put the salad on the table." Gabby came in with Karma trailing behind her.

I grabbed a trivet to put under the lasagna. Khalan put the lasagna on top of it and looked around. "Where should I sit?"

"By me." Gabby pulled out a chair at the head of the table. "You can sit here, and me and Arianna can sit on either side of you." She looked at me. "Sorry, Mom, but you can't sit beside him."

I laughed and sat down beside Arianna. "I understand."

I watched as everyone heaped their plates.

After my divorce, I hadn't known if I would ever feel like I had my family back together again.

But now, in this moment, with my girls and Khalan all sitting together, everything finally felt like it was going to be okay.

*A*fter dinner, Khalan helped with the dishes while Arianna took the dog to the backyard. Khalan had made an effort to eat in front of the girls, but I'd caught him sneaking his food to Karma.

"I know what you are." Gabby crossed her arms over her chest and stared at him.

"What?" He jerked his head in her direction and glanced over at me.

"I know you're a wizard." Gabby smirked.

"Ah." His expression relaxed, and he went back to drying the skillet.

"Do you have a wand?" Gabby cocked her head.

"No, I don't." He gave a ghost of a smile.

"But I thought all wizards had wands."

"Not necessarily. I find it's just one more thing to carry." Khalan shrugged. I snorted.

Arianna came running into the kitchen. "Mom! You aren't going to believe this. Scooby is in the back yard again."

"Great." I dried my hands on the dishtowel and headed to the back yard. Khalan and the girls followed.

Karma was barking his head off. Scooby was trying to hump the German Shepherd but was too short. So, he settled for trying to hump Karma's leg.

Karma wasn't amused and continued to bark and snap at the little dog.

"Stop that!" I yelled. "Scooby, stop that right now."

I knew I had the ability to glamour animals, but they had to be looking at me. Scooby was focused on Karma's back leg and wouldn't even make eye contact with me.

"I'll get the hose and get Scooby off."

"Wait. Let Khalan do some wizardly magic." Gabby grabbed my arm.

"Gabby, honey…"

"She's right. I'll take care of it." Khalan walked towards the dogs. As soon as Karma saw him approach, he stopped snapping at Scooby.

Khalan squatted in front of Scooby, who was still humping Karma's leg.

He made eye contact with Scooby and waved his fingers in the air. "Stop humping the German Shepherd."

Immediately, Scooby ceased his sexual activity. He cocked his head to the side and studied Khalan.

"I want you to go home and stop bothering the dogs in the neighborhood." He waved his fingers as he spoke.

Khalan stood, and Scooby stepped back from Karma. He trotted over to the fence and squeezed his little body through.

"See! I told you he was a wizard." Gabby squealed with delight.

"I'd say a dog whisperer." Arianna laughed.

"Don't tell anyone. It's a secret." Khalan walked over to us.

"We promise not to tell anyone," Gabby said solemnly. Arianna nodded in agreement.

The girls and the dog headed inside, which left me alone with Khalan.

I turned and looked into his eyes. "Thank you for the dog. The girls love him."

"Good. He needed a good home." He took a step closer.

My heart beat faster.

"You were gone when I woke up." I felt my cheeks heat.

"I had some things to do." He laced his fingers through mine and stared into my eyes.

"Where did you get the dog?"

"He was abandoned by his owners when they moved. I found him chained to a tree in the back yard. I took him to live with me until he got stronger. He was skin and bones when I found him."

"How can anyone abandon an animal like that?"

"Humans are like that." Khalan arched a brow.

"I'm not like that." I pouted.

"You're not human." He traced his finger across my lips.

My lips parted at his touch. "My girls are human."

"Your girls are very much like their mother. Extraordinary." His hand cupped my cheek.

The back door opened, and Arianna stuck her head out. I took a step away from Khalan.

"You guys can stop all the sneaking around. We already know you're an item," Arianna deadpanned.

"What?" I stared at her.

"Give it up, Mom." She walked outside and propped her hands on her hips. "We aren't stupid. We know you two are dating."

I opened my mouth but didn't know what to say.

Khalan turned and met my daughter's gaze. "Arianna, I actually came over here tonight to ask for your and Gabby's permission to date your mom."

"You did?" I gaped at him. My heart warmed at his words.

I didn't have a name to fit all the emotions swimming around inside of me.

"Yes." He looked at me, then he turned back to Arianna.

"What's going on out here?" Gabby yelled from the back door. "Whatever it is, don't leave me out." She ran over with Karma on her heels.

"Gabby, I would like to ask you and Arianna for permission to date your mom." Khalan looked from one to the other.

"Of course, you can. We've never had a wizard in the family." She wrapped her arms around his waist and gave him a hug. After she'd let go, she came over and gave me a hug before heading into the house with the dog.

"Arianna?" I couldn't help but feel nervous at what she was going to say.

"As long as you make my mom happy, then I fully support it." Arianna stepped up to Khalan and gave him a quick side hug. "I better go make sure Gabby isn't feeding the dog chocolate." She jogged back into the house.

I was speechless.

"Well, that went better than I expected." Khalan looked at me.

"Are you kidding? Arianna hugged you." I gaped.

"It was more of a side hug." He shrugged.

"You don't understand. She hugs *no one*. When I go in for a hug, it's like hugging a limp ragdoll. And I have yet to see her hug Miles goodbye when he drops them off. I'm telling you, this is huge."

"Well, don't start signing me up for the father and daughter dance at school. She'll probably change her mind by tomorrow and hate me. Like a typical teenager."

"Maybe." I studied him. I had seen him wipe his eye when she hugged him. He wasn't as aloof as he was letting on.

"So, what do you say we watch a movie with the girls?" I walked up to him and slid my hands up his chest.

He cupped my butt and held me close. "And after they go to sleep, we'll do something incredibly naughty behind your locked bedroom door." He brought his mouth down across mine and kissed me long and hard. I melted against him and wrapped my arms around his neck.

When he finally broke the kiss, we were both breathing hard.

"Better get inside before I pull you into the woods and have my way with you." His husky voice sent chills down my back.

"We have time for a quickie." I brightened.

Arianna threw open the back door. "Mom, Gabby won't give me the remote control."

I sighed. "We're coming."

CHAPTER 36

I woke up to the shrill sound of my cell phone ringing.

I patted the nightstand and grabbed the offensive object. I cracked open an eye. Sunlight was streaming in the window. I had forgotten to close the curtains after getting home from dropping the girls off at school.

"Hello?"

"Rachel. This is Gina. You are never going to believe this…"

"What time is it?"

"It's noon. Are you asleep? What's wrong? Do you have the flu or something?"

"I'm fine. I just stayed up late last night, so I took a nap." It wasn't exactly a lie. "What's going on?" I sat up and rubbed my eyes.

"The riverboat that hosted the Aces and Eights charity party ended up hitting something in the Mississippi River. Tore a hole in the hull."

"Oh, yeah?" I yawned.

"They sent divers down to fix it and guess what they found?"

"I don't know, Gina." I was too tired to pay attention.

"They found Brad's truck. With his body still inside."

My eyes sprang open, and I gasped. "What?"

"I know! I can't believe it either. I bet Nikki is excited to finally get her life insurance money."

"So, he did kill himself?" My voice trembled.

"Oh, Rachel. I'm so sorry. I know you were friends with him, too. I didn't mean to spring this on you so suddenly."

"No, it's okay. I mean, it's shocking. And horrible. I guess Brad did kill himself."

"That's the thing. They did an autopsy. There was no water in his lungs. Which means, he didn't drown himself in the river."

"So, how did he die?"

"Well, it's hard to say. They said there was trauma to his face and neck. But he's been in the water a while, and they said the fish had been eating him. They're still trying to figure out the cause of death."

"Did they find anything else?" I prayed to God my DNA wasn't anywhere on him or his truck. Surely, the water would have washed it all away...

"I don't know. But I will keep you updated when I get any other news."

"Thanks, I appreciate it."

"Again, I'm sorry, Rachel." Gina ended the call.

Just when things were looking up, I had to deal with murder.

ABOUT THE AUTHOR

Jodi Vaughn is an USA TODAY Best-selling Southern Paranormal Romance author. When she's not busy playing with her characters and typing away at her laptop, she can be found enjoying a cup of tea (or a very large glass of wine) in her home in Northeast Arkansas. She resides in Arkansas with her family, three dogs, and two fickle swans who travel the neighborhood in search of greener pastures.

Newsletter sign up!

Cloverton Series

Christmas in Cloverton

Lost Without You (book 1)

Lost All Control (book 2)

Made in the USA
Middletown, DE
08 June 2020